"You Play Dirty."

He didn't even bat an eye. "Only when it counts."

"Why do I get the feeling it counts a lot?"

"I play to win."

"This isn't a game, Lucas." A little girl's future was on the line. Amelia wasn't some pawn to be passed around at the whim and convenience of the adults in her life.

He paused for a moment, expression hardening, obviously taking offense at Devin's candor. "That's why it counts." He rapped his knuckles decisively on the tabletop. "How long will it take you to move in?"

Dear Reader,

One of the greatest things about writing a baby book is the chance to relive cherished memories. There's nothing quite like bringing that first wee one home from the hospital, then muddling your way through feeding, diapering and sleep schedules. The idea for *Billionaire Baby Dilemma* came from remembering all those new dads valiantly learning the ropes.

In *Billionaire Baby Dilemma,* Lucas Demarco is thrown reluctantly into the role of daddy. Where mothering comes naturally to Devin Hartley, at first all Lucas can see is a smelly, sticky, squirmy little package of noise. That is, until baby Amelia weaves her way into his heart.

I hope you enjoy *Billionaire Baby Dilemma.* It was a pleasure to write!

Happy reading,

Barbara Dunlop

BARBARA DUNLOP

BILLIONAIRE BABY DILEMMA

Silhouette® Desire

Published by Silhouette Books

America's Publisher of Contemporary Romance

For Karen and Martin.

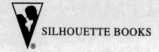

SILHOUETTE BOOKS

ISBN-13: 978-0-373-73086-5

BILLIONAIRE BABY DILEMMA

Recycling programs
for this product may
not exist in your area.

Visit Silhouette Books at www.eHarlequin.com

Printed in U.S.A.

Books by Barbara Dunlop

Silhouette Desire

BARBARA DUNLOP

writes romantic stories while curled up in a log cabin in Canada's far north, where bears outnumber people and it snows six months of the year. Fortunately she has a brawny husband and two teenage children to haul firewood and clear the driveway while she sips cocoa and muses about her upcoming chapters. Barbara loves to hear from readers. You can contact her through her website at www.barbaradunlop.com.

Dear Reader,

Yes, it's true. We're changing our name! After more than twenty-five years of being part of Harlequin Enterprises, Silhouette Books will officially seal the merger by taking the company's name.

So if you notice a few changes on the covers starting April 2011—Silhouette Special Edition becoming Harlequin Special Edition, Silhouette Desire becoming Harlequin Desire, and Silhouette Romantic Suspense becoming Harlequin Romantic Suspense—don't be concerned.

We'll continue to have the same fantastic authors, wonderful stories, eye-catching covers and emotional, compelling reads. We're just going to be moving under the overall company name, which will make us even easier for you to see in the stores, on the internet and wherever you usually find us!

So look for the new logo, but remember, beneath the image will be the same promise of romantic stories of love, passion, adventure, family and a whole lot more. Just the way you like them!

Sincerely,

The Editors at Harlequin Books

One

Lucas Demarco was a man who liked certainty. He liked concretes, and he liked control. What his cousin Steve Foster was proposing lacked every one of those essential elements.

"Primarily Brazil," Steve was saying. "But East Palites is a free trade zone for all of South America. Pacific Robotics would be in on the ground floor for high tech."

Lucas hoisted his dripping wet sea kayak and paddle over his head and started back up the short path from the family's private dock on Puget Sound to their boathouse. "The political situation is far too unstable."

"They're not going to nationalize the high-tech sector," Steve countered, as he followed along in business suit and a pair of loafers. "That would be suicide."

Lucas flipped the kayak onto the grass outside the boathouse and uncoiled a garden hose. "Right. Because lunatic dictators always make rational decisions."

"If we don't do this, Lucas, somebody else will."

"Let them," said Lucas, unzipping his life jacket and slipping it off over his wet suit. It was a warm May evening, but the ocean temperature was still cold enough to turn a person hypothermic. "I don't mind being second into a market like that."

Steve's hands went to his hips, wrinkling his dark suit jacket. "This *isn't* your decision."

"It isn't yours, either. And a stalemate means we stick with the status quo." And that was fine for this particular stalemate. But Lucas knew they had to resolve the situation around his orphaned, baby niece Amelia, and they'd have to do it very soon.

He and Steve each owned forty-five percent of Pacific Robotics, making Amelia's ten percent the key to the corporation.

Lucas knew it, and Steve knew it, and so did several dozen lawyers, company executives and competitors. Whoever controlled Amelia was the swing vote in every Pacific Robotics corporate decision from here on in.

Both Lucas and his brother Konrad had put their hearts and souls into the billion dollar corporation. As long as Konrad was alive and in control of his daughter's shares, both Amelia and the corporation were safe. But with Konrad's death, Lucas needed permanent guardianship of the baby girl in order to have deciding control. It was the only way to protect her from outside corporate vultures who'd try to use her, and the only way to ensure the future of Pacific Robotics.

"You son of a bitch," growled Steve.

Lucas shrugged and spun the outside tap, pointing the stream of water at the kayak's deck to hose off the salt. "Lucky my mother's not alive to hear you say that."

"I'll fight Granddad's will," Steve vowed, raising his voice. "Don't you think I won't prove what Konrad did."

"Konrad got married and had a baby," said Lucas, squelching the shot of pain that came with uttering his dead brother's name. By fathering Amelia, Konrad had met the conditions of their grandfather's will and secured the family inheritance for the Demarco side of the family, instead of the irresponsible risk-taking Fosters, who were more interested in jet-setting vacations than annual reports and balance sheets.

Though Lucas had his own concerns about the speed with which Konrad had fallen in love and married Monica Hartley, he'd never share them with Steve. And he was confident that Konrad had at the very least been well on his way to loving her when they got married.

In any event, it was a moot point. As the firstborn, Amelia was their grandfather's heir. Steve had already insisted on a DNA test, and it had proven Konrad was Amelia's father.

Lucas flipped the kayak over and began hosing down the bright blue hull.

"So, when's the temporary guardianship hearing?" asked Steve, the change in his tone putting Lucas on alert.

Monica had died in the light plane crash along with Konrad, and her sister—Devin Hartley—was fighting Lucas for guardianship of Amelia.

"Next week," Lucas answered, glancing up.

Steve nodded, a calculating look entering his eyes. "And, if Devin wins?"

Bingo. There it was.

"You stay away from Devin," Lucas warned, sending Steve a dark look. Not that he intended to lose. Not that he expected Devin to be a factor in the long term.

Steve's gaze wandered to the sun setting over the mountains of Bainbridge Island. "It's a free country," he mused in a calculating tone.

"I mean it," said Lucas, cranking off the tap. "It is not open season on Devin Hartley."

She seemed like a decent woman, a little bohemian and flighty, and definitely more emotional than Lucas would have liked. Still, he couldn't help remembering there was something inherently sensual about the way she moved and the way she smiled. Her blue eyes had sparkled that night at Konrad's wedding, as if she were hiding a secret, and he found himself wanting to discover it.

He knew that his reaction had been ridiculous. And he'd eventually discounted the memory. Until now. Not that it mattered one way or the other. Bottom line, he was not about to stand by and let Steve cozy up to her in the hope of opening up a division of Pacific Robotics in South America.

Steve's smile was sly and confident. "If she wins, there is no way to stop me from presenting my case."

Lucas jerked the rubber hose back into a coil. "And you called me a son of a bitch."

"In this instance, I call you cowardly and unimaginative."

Lucas stuffed the hose back on the wall bracket. "And I call you reckless."

"So, we agree to disagree?"

"Stay away from Devin."

"Seriously, Lucas. Who died and left you king?"

"Granddad."

"No. He died and left Konrad king." Steve gave a thoughtful pause. "And, you know, I could have lived with that."

Lucas dragged down the zipper of his wet suit, trying not to be surprised by the unvarnished, frontal attack. "Are you saying you wish I'd died instead?"

"I'm saying Konrad was the better man. He was like me. He knew how the game was played."

"Konrad was nothing like you." Konrad might have had a reckless streak, but he wasn't devious and conniving. Lucas could trust his brother to be honest and to operate in the best interest of the family. Steve could only be trusted to look out for his own tainted agenda.

Steve took a step forward, leaning in, eyes narrowing. "This is an era of global diversification, Lucas. We need to expand. Those who do will thrive. Those who don't will wither and die."

"And those who lose their industrial assets to a military coup?"

"At least they had the gonads to try."

Lucas stripped out of the tight, black wet suit and hung it up on the outside rack. "There's a difference between bravery and reckless stupidity."

Steve shook his head as he scoffed out a laugh. "That's just what the cowards tell themselves."

Lucas tamped down his frustration. At the same time, he battled a brief burst of loneliness. Steve had been a jerk for most of his life, but Konrad had always been around to help turn Steve's behavior into a joke.

Lucas and Konrad had each led their own lives, there was no doubt about that. Konrad had spent most of his time at his apartment in Bellevue. And for the past year, he'd been pretty obsessed with getting his estranged wife back into his life. But until he'd lost his brother, Lucas hadn't realized how much he counted on having someone around who understood the pressures and conflicts of running the company, someone who could laugh at the foibles of relatives who were tied so closely together through the family business.

"You might want to man up on this," said Steve.

"And you might want to start using your brain instead of relying on blind ambition."

"Then I guess I'll see you in court."

"You're not invited."

"It's a free country," Steve repeated, the words clearly a challenge.

When Lucas refused to react, Steve shook his head and turned up the path to the mansion.

Lucas jerked out six feet of hose and turned the spray on his wet suit.

He'd struggled most of his life not to flatten his annoying cousin. Konrad had always been the diplomat of the family, convincing a teenage Lucas that he couldn't win against Steve by using his fists. But with Konrad gone, and no buffer left between them, Lucas was sorely tempted to try.

With Amelia finally down for her nap, Devin Hartley moved through the living room of her lakeside cottage, picking up plastic toys, blankets and the assorted books and magazines that had been strewn around the room. Since Amelia had started to crawl last month, she'd been pulling up on the furniture, and even taking the odd shaky step while she held on to the furniture, so Devin had baby-proofed the lower three feet of the house. Still, by noon most days, the place looked like a war zone.

"All quiet?" It was her neighbor Lexi's soft voice, as she carefully slid open the screen door from the deck.

Devin smiled and motioned Lexi inside. The woman was in her early forties, with three grown children who'd all left the state for either jobs or college.

Lexi had lost her husband six years ago in a boating accident. And it was her empathy and understanding that got Devin through those first terrible weeks after Monica and Konrad's plane had crashed.

"Get any sleep last night?" asked Lexi, sliding the door shut behind her. The mosquitoes were out already, and the bumblebees who were attracted to the gardens and wildflowers were beginning to make their presence known.

"Six straight hours," Devin bragged with a self-satisfied smile. Sleep was a rare commodity these days.

Lexi bent to pick up the closest toys and deposited them into the brightly colored wooden box in the corner of the room.

Devin's decor was nothing to get excited about—two burgundy armchairs, a striped couch and various mismatched tables and lamps. The small, stone fireplace hadn't been used in years, while the rose-colored carpet had a distinct traffic pattern into the kitchen and out onto the deck that overlooked the lake.

But it was clean and cozy, and Devin loved her little cottage. It was the perfect place for Amelia to play, and if bits of dirt and sand were tracked in from the lake, nobody cared. The bedrooms were compact, while the kitchen was bright and cheerful. For most of the year, it was warm enough to eat on the deck, and Devin had splurged last year on a gorgeous table and padded chairs, with matching loungers and a big gas barbecue.

"You have time for tea?" asked Lexi.

"Absolutely." Devin hoped Amelia would sleep for at least an hour.

"Anything new on temporary guardianship?"

"Only that I'm dreading the hearing." Devin sighed, tossing the last few blocks into their plastic tube then sealing the lid. "I don't know why can't we just leave things the way they are."

It was less than two months until the hearing for permanent guardianship of Amelia, but for some reason Lucas Demarco had suddenly decided he wanted temporary custody. His lawyers had sent a threatening letter, forcing Devin into court next week.

"You know why he's doing it." Lexi arched a brow as she shook out a yellow flannel, baby blanket and folded it in half.

"Yes, I do."

"To get close to Amelia."

Devin nodded her agreement. "It's my big advantage over him at the moment."

"Good luck to him, I say." Lexi stacked the blanket on top of three others on the back of the sofa. "He's hardly daddy material."

Lexi had only met Lucas once, at Monica's wedding. But they'd both read stories about his exploits as a cold-blooded businessman and a sexy, jet-setting bachelor. It was obvious to anyone with a brain that Lucas was only interested in Amelia because the baby girl had inherited shares in Pacific Robotics. And controlling her would give Lucas fifty-five percent of the company, so his decisions would be final.

Most of the time, Devin was confident that any judge would see right through his scheme. But every once in a while, in the middle of night when her confidence was low and life seemed overwhelming, Devin feared Lucas might actually win the case and take Amelia away.

As Lexi headed for the kitchen, Devin shook off the fear. She snagged the last of the baby dolls, straightened a stack of magazines and pulled the rolling ottoman back into its place.

A knock sounded on the door that was tucked in a foyer at the back of the living room.

Lexi peeked around the kitchen wall, brows going up in surprise. Nobody knocked on Devin's door. In the close-knit community of Lake Westmire, people usually crossed to the front deck, opened the glass slider and walked in. If they wanted to be formal, they might call out before entering.

Feeling slightly self-conscious in her faded T-shirt, worn blue jeans and bare feet, Devin made her way to the back of the house. She took a glance through the small, rectangular window and vaguely recognized the man standing on the porch. She opened the door halfway and tried to pinpoint what was familiar about him.

He was about five foot eight, with medium-length, reddish blond hair. He wore a dark suit with a pale blue, accent-striped shirt and a navy tie. He looked to be in his midthirties, although his round face gave him a perpetual boyish look. And the light-colored eyebrows didn't help.

"Can I help you?" She kept her voice low so she wouldn't disturb Amelia.

The man stuck out his hand and offered a friendly, salesman-like smile. "Steve Foster. We met at Konrad and Monica's wedding." The smile promptly disappeared. "Allow me to express my condolences for your loss."

"Thank you," Devin automatically responded, taking his hand while clicking through her memory for his face.

Then she got it. Right. Steve Foster. He was Konrad's cousin. She drew back her hand and pressed her lips together.

"I'm sorry for your loss, too," she responded, although she held the entire Demarco family partially responsible for her sister's death. If they all hadn't been so greedy and distrustful, they wouldn't have panicked over Amelia's shares. Konrad wouldn't have been so desperate to win Monica back, and Monica never would have got on the plane that night.

"I hope I'm not disturbing you," he continued affably.

"Is there something you need?" Her tone had cooled, and she could hear Lexi in the living room behind her, moving in closer, presumably to take stock of the situation.

"I came to apologize," he offered. "On behalf of my family. I understand Lucas has been harassing you."

Devin didn't know what to say to that. Lucas was the current bane of her existence. But she wasn't exactly sure what Steve was apologizing for, nor what he meant by "harassing."

The kettle squealed behind her, and Lexi's footsteps swiftly disappeared into the kitchen.

"I only just learned about the temporary guardianship hearing."

Well, that answered one question.

But she still didn't know why he was here.

Steve cleared his throat. "Would you mind terribly if I…" He gestured inside her house. "I have an offer for you."

"I'm not interested," said Devin. She didn't trust any of the Demarcos, or the Fosters, particularly when they were pretending to be nice.

"I'd like to make up for Lucas's actions."

Devin canted her head to one side, attempting to judge the expression in his pale blue eyes. "Why?" she challenged.

He appeared contrite and guileless. "Because he's treating you badly. He's got five very expensive lawyers on the case. I know these guys and, quite frankly, Devin, you don't stand a chance."

A cold fear hit the pit of Devin's stomach. Added to it was a rush of suspicion. There was no reason in the world for Steve to warn her about Lucas. The Demarco family wanted Amelia, and Steve was one of them.

"What do you want?" she demanded, assuming he was up to no good.

"I just told you." He met her gaze straight on, without so much as a blink. If this was an act, he was very good.

She allowed for the slim possibility that he was being honest. "Why would you care?"

Devin heard Lexi come closer behind her. It warmed Devin's heart to know Lexi was on her side. Not that Lexi was a lawyer, and not that Lexi was in any better position than Devin to hire an expensive law firm.

"I care, because I'm a decent human being. And I'm doing more than just warning you. I'm here to offer you the services of a first-class law firm. I have Bernard and Botlow on retainer, and you're welcome to use them for the hearing next week. Free of charge, of course."

Devin blinked at the man.

Lexi pulled the door wider. "What's the catch?"

Steve saw Lexi, and his expression faltered for a split second. "Hello. And you are?"

"I'm a friend of Devin's."

He turned his attention back to Devin. "Do you mind if I come in for a moment?"

"The baby's asleep," she told him.

"I'll be very quiet." He waited, then he looked to Lexi. "I'm here to offer legal services, nothing more. You can check out the law firm, check out the lawyers. They have an excellent reputation, and I won't be in any way remotely involved in the case."

He looked back at Devin. "My cousin is treating you unfairly. He's stacked the deck in his favor, and I want to level the playing field."

Devin didn't like to think about Steve's cousin Lucas. He was a Demarco through and through. And that meant he was devastatingly handsome, sexy, self-assured and powerful. The combination should have been annoying. It *was* annoying. But it was also arousing in a knee-jerk, anthropological sort of way, and Devin found herself having to guard against a sexual attraction to the man who was growing more aggravating by the day. She thought about her overworked, sole proprietor lawyer down on Beach Drive. Hannah was wonderful. She was bright and hardworking, and she'd cut her fees considerably for Devin. But she wasn't a family law specialist.

"You can always say no to me inside," Steve offered reasonably.

Devin glanced at Lexi. The woman gave a nearly imperceptible shrug, and Devin decided to take a chance. After all, Steve was right about one thing. She could say no to him in her living room as well as she could say it on the porch. There seemed little risk in listening to what he had to say.

Lucas knew that LoJacking Steve's car brought him dangerously close to the line ethics-wise. But when the device went still for half an hour out at Lake Westmire, he knew his suspicions were confirmed and his actions justified.

He left the mansion through the front foyer, crossing the

driveway turnaround to the garage that housed his jet-black Bugatti.

He cut the hour-long drive down to forty minutes, passing the blip that signaled Steve's Porsche coming the other way along the interstate south of Seattle. His GPS took him down the winding, beachfront road of Lake Westmire, unerringly to a gravel driveway behind a compact, white cottage that obviously fronted on the lake.

He yanked the parking brake, killed the engine and exited the low-slung vehicle.

The staircase was short, and it brought him to a narrow wraparound deck that most likely led to a veranda overlooking the lake. Facing the road, there was a painted, blue door. He knocked.

After a few minutes, Devin peeped through the small window, frowning before she opened the door to him.

"Lucas?" She glanced both ways, checking for what, he didn't know, but obviously puzzled by his presence.

"What did he want?" Lucas asked without preamble, hoping a strong offense would put her off balance.

"Excuse me?"

"Steve," Lucas continued, taking advantage of the small opening she'd left between her body and the entry wall to barrel inside.

She took a reflexive step backward, the action opening the door wider. "I have no idea what you're talking about."

Lucas turned and braced himself against the painted, yellow wall in the small entry, leaving eighteen inches or so between them. He was disappointed that she'd lie outright. Then again, what did he know about her?

"Steve was here," he stated.

She didn't answer.

"Is that the way you want to play this?" he persisted. "Are you going to look me square in the eyes and lie?"

Her expression faltered for a second, but she blinked her long lashes over her deep blue eyes, camouflaging her feelings. "What are you doing here?"

"Tell me what he wanted. Did he plead his case? Try to make a deal?" If Lucas understood Steve's tactics, he'd be in a better position to counteract them.

"You're not making sense."

He pinned her with a glare. "I saw his car."

"You were *spying* on me?"

"No." In point of fact, he'd been spying on Steve. "I was not spying on you. But I know he was here, and I want to know what he told you."

Opening a manufacturing plant in South America was not a decision to be taken lightly. Steve would have given her a rosy profit picture and glossed over all the risks. It made Lucas crazy that he had to justify his international corporate strategy to a woman whose sole business experience was in autographing her trite, self-help books for the lovelorn.

Devin gave her head a little shake, her short, wispy, brunette hair moving ever so slightly with the motion. "It's none of your business."

Lucas felt his blood pressure rise. "So, you admit he was here."

"That's also none of your business."

"Damn it, Devin," he shouted.

A baby's cry sounded from farther inside the house.

Devin smacked the palm of her hand against the end of the open door. "Now see what you've done?"

Lucas instantly realized Amelia was here.

Of course Amelia was here. She lived here.

Devin turned on her heel and swished into the living room on bare feet, her faded jeans clinging to a shapely rear end. Lucas ignored the view. Instead, he took the opportunity to close the door and follow her inside the house. He wasn't leaving without answers.

Devin reemerged into the living room, a red-faced, blubbering and soggy-looking Amelia tucked over one shoulder. Her hand rubbed up and down the baby's back as she snarled at Lucas. "Thanks tons."

"I didn't know she was sleeping."

"It's three in the afternoon. What did you think she'd be doing?"

Lucas didn't have a clue, and it seemed pointless to venture a guess. "If you'll just tell me what Steve said."

Amelia's cries grew louder, and Devin began jiggling her. "You have a lot of nerve, Lucas Demarco. Barging in here—"

"Steve has a lot of nerve sneaking around behind my back."

She stilled. "He offered to help me."

Lucas snorted out a cold laugh. "Steve's never helped anybody his entire life."

Amelia shrieked, nearly piercing Lucas's eardrums. He cut her an annoyed glance. "Can't you do something to—"

To his shock, Devin plopped the baby against his chest.

He automatically reached out to grasp the child beneath her arms, leaving her dangling out of the way of his clean suit. "What the…"

"You try," said Devin.

Amelia took one look at Lucas's face and opened her mouth to bawl. Her eyes scrunched shut, tears squeezing out the corners, and her face turned brighter red as the decibels increased.

Devin headed for the kitchen.

"Where are you going?" Lucas cried, embarrassed by the high pitch to his voice.

"To get her a bottle."

"But—" The baby squirmed against his grip, but he was afraid to hold her closer. Her nose was running, and shiny drool was smeared across her chin.

He was wearing a Savile Row suit, for pity's sake.

Then she suddenly stopped howling. She stiffened. Her face scrunched up, and a horrible rumble emanated from her little body. The stench that filled the air nearly made him gag. He breathed shallowly, through his mouth, glancing frantically around the room for a place to put her down.

Thankfully, Devin emerged from the kitchen.

"That's a good girl," she cooed, shooting Lucas a glare,

retrieving the baby and cuddling her close, barely flinching at the smell.

Lucas took a very large step backward, silently acknowledging Devin's fortitude.

"Do you need a change, sweetheart?" she asked the baby.

Lucas thought fumigation might be more in order. But when Devin laid Amelia on her back on the floor and reached for a bright blue diaper bag, all he could think about was escaping.

He darted toward an open window.

"Would you like to change her?" Devin asked sweetly.

Lucas's jaw dropped open. He could probably count on one hand the number of times in his life he'd been rendered speechless. But this was one of them.

"Since you're going for sole custody," Devin continued, "you might as well get in some practice."

"She'll have a nanny," he pointed out.

Devin tugged off Amelia's stretchy pink pants, revealing a white diaper. "You don't plan to change her diapers?"

Lucas turned away, gazing across the wooden deck and the sloped lawn to the calm waters of the lake. Devin's neighbor had a dock with a sleek speedboat tied up. A few dozen houses were visible along the curve of the shoreline, front yards neatly landscaped, while evergreens covered the hillsides behind. It was actually quite beautiful here.

"Lucas?" Devin prompted.

"I don't expect it to be necessary," he said, answering her question. There was a very good reason why nannies were invented.

"There's a girl," Devin cooed, and Lucas dared to look back to where Amelia stood on chubby bare feet, hand grasping Devin's hair for balance.

Devin tucked away the change pad and handed Amelia a bottle of juice. The baby promptly plunked down on her fresh diaper and popped the bottle in her mouth.

"Why do you want custody?" Devin asked, coming to her feet, brushing her palms across her backside and finger-combing her hair where Amelia had mussed it. Her T-shirt was wrinkled, and several damp spots dotted its front. It was no wonder she went for plain, serviceable clothing. He could only imagine the havoc Amelia would wreak on linen and silk.

Still, the plain clothing couldn't hide her gorgeous figure. She was short, maybe five-five. And the absence of heels made her seem even shorter. But her legs were lithe and toned, her waist nipped in and breasts rounded and in perfect proportion to everything else.

He didn't know what she did for exercise, but it was working.

"You don't seem particularly interested in Amelia," Devin continued.

"She's a Demarco."

"So?"

"So, I have a responsibility—"

"Can't you at least be honest?"

"I am being honest." He owed it to his brother to keep Amelia safe. If Lucas had died with a daughter in such a vulnerable position, he'd expect no less of Konrad.

"You want her ten percent of Pacific Robotics, Lucas, controlling interest. You don't give one whit about Amelia as a person."

"You're dead wrong about that."

"I'll do whatever you ask for the company," she pledged. "I promise I won't interfere."

He wished he could believe her. "What did Steve say?"

"I can't tell you that."

Lucas threw up his hands. "I *know* what he said." He'd offered her a deal. If she won guardianship of Amelia, Steve would make it worth her while to support his plans for expansion into South America.

"Then why ask me?"

"I wanted to know if I could trust you."

She moved closer. "You're lying. You'll never trust me. You wanted information to use against me."

She was close.

He'd wanted information to use against Steve. "I can see this is getting us nowhere."

"I'm way ahead of you, Lucas. I've known for weeks that we were going nowhere."

He gazed into her crystal blue eyes, unable to help noticing her dark lashes, prettily arched brows, small, straight nose, bow lips and creamy smooth skin. She was a beautiful woman. She was also feisty and passionate, making her a frustrating opponent.

But he'd defeated frustrating opponents before. And he'd win this battle, too. She might know how to change a diaper, but Amelia needed more than hugs and a fresh bottom. She was a Demarco. She would one day control a significant percentage of a corporation worth hundreds of millions of dollars.

She needed education, advice and experience, and she needed the security and savvy that went along with her future position in life. Lake Westmire might be a fine place to raise most children. But it wasn't enough for Amelia.

Two

Devin was more than pleased with the lawyer Steve had provided for the temporary custody hearing. The man made his points to the judge concisely and eloquently, describing Devin's bond with Amelia, how Devin had been present during her birth and that Amelia had lived in Devin's house since coming home from the hospital. He provided testimonial letters from friends and neighbors speaking of Devin's parenting skills, the nursery she'd outfitted for Amelia and her attention to Amelia's health and well-being.

He'd then contrasted Lucas's lack of parenting experience, his plans to hire a nanny instead of being hands-on himself and the fact that he'd spent almost no time with Amelia since her birth. He acknowledged the security concerns around a child from such a wealthy family, but pointed out there were many options to ensure her safety.

Devin had to admit, she'd never thought about the potential of someone kidnapping Amelia for ransom. Did that even still happen in America? It had been a long time since the Lindbergh case.

She'd thought he'd done a stellar job, thought they were sure to win. But then at the last minute Lucas's lawyer stood up to address the judge.

He acknowledged Devin's bond with Amelia, talked about the portability of Devin's career as a self-help book writer, then suggested what he called a compromise—that both Amelia and Devin take up temporary residence at the Demarco mansion. Amelia could be with Devin, but she'd also have the advantage of the Demarco security.

Devin's gaze flew to Lucas's face. His smug expression told her he'd planned this all along.

He'd known he couldn't beat her in a straight-up fight, and he'd come up with an underhanded way to snatch her victory. By the time permanent guardianship was considered, Lucas would have built a bond with Amelia. And Devin's best advantage would be gone.

She opened her mouth to protest, but she knew there was no way out. Any argument she put forward would make her sound unreasonable. This same judge would eventually decide permanent guardianship, and Devin couldn't afford to yield the moral high ground to Lucas. On the face of it, he was offering a reasonable solution.

In reality, he had outmaneuvered her. Amelia would be under his roof, and under his care, and Devin knew he would pull out all the stops to make the Demarco mansion a perfect home for the baby.

"Ms. Hartley?" asked the judge, her hand going to the gavel.

Devin's lawyer spoke up. "We can't support that kind of disruption to Amelia's life. She's already lost her mother. Ms. Hartley's house is the only home she's ever known."

The judge's gaze moved to Devin. "You're a writer? You work from home?"

Devin had no choice but to nod.

"Do you have other children?"

Devin shook her head.

"Do you object to coming to a compromise?"

Devin recognized a trick question when she heard it. Next, the judge would want to know why she objected to better security for Amelia. She shook her head in capitulation.

The judge brought the gavel down. "So ordered. Temporary custody goes to Ms. Hartley, provided she and the child reside at the Demarco mansion. Open visitation is awarded to Mr. Demarco. I trust you will arrange for security, sir?"

"Of course, Your Honor." Lucas nodded.

Devin's lawyer leaned sideways. "Sorry about that."

Devin shook her head. "You couldn't have seen it coming."

"Lucas is a good strategist."

Devin scoffed. "In my neighborhood, we call that conniving."

"That's what we call it in my neighborhood, too." He placed the file folders back in his briefcase. "But it works."

"It works," Devin agreed. And she had no one to blame but herself. She'd underestimated Lucas. She'd make sure that never happened again.

"Devin?" Lucas stepped across the courtroom to her table, his shadow coming over her.

"You're a piece of work," she said as she gathered her purse and pushed back her chair.

"So I've been told."

"You backed me into a corner."

"Yes, I did."

Devin looked up. "You play dirty."

He didn't even bat an eye. "Only when it counts."

"Why do I get the feeling it counts a lot?"

"I play to win."

"This isn't a game, Lucas." A little girl's future was on the line. Amelia wasn't some pawn to be passed around at the whim and convenience of the adults in her life.

He paused for a moment, expression hardening, obviously taking offense at Devin's candor. "That's why it counts." He rapped his knuckles decisively on the tabletop. "How long will it take you to pack?"

She stood to confront him. She'd worn two-inch heels, but she wished she had a little more height. He was easily over six feet, neatly trimmed hair, freshly shaved, an expensive suit, fine silk tie, everything pressed to within an inch of its life. The man positively reeked power.

"You mean in days?" she asked sarcastically, thinking she'd need a couple of weeks.

"I meant in hours."

She did an expression check to see if he was joking. He wasn't.

"When you say jump, do people generally ask how high?"

He tented his fingers on the table and leaned slightly forward. "I try not to say jump unless I have to."

She refused to flinch under his attempt at intimidation. "I need a week."

"No problem."

She blinked in surprise.

"I'll take Amelia with me now, and you can catch up."

"Don't be ridiculous."

Lucas turned to Devin's lawyer, who had been watching the exchange with obvious interest. "Bill? Is there a countdown to the judge's order? Some sort of implementation period?"

Devin looked to Bill. "No countdown," he admitted with an apologetic glance in Devin's direction. "The order takes effect right away."

Lucas turned his attention back to Devin. "How long will it take you to pack?" he repeated.

She couldn't let him win again. Certainly not this early, and definitely not this decisively. She frantically searched her brain for a comeback.

Then it came to her, and her shoulders relaxed with relief. The man was bluffing.

Instead of answering his question, she reached into her purse for her cell phone, flipped it open and pressed the speed dial for Lexi.

Lexi picked up after a single ring. "How'd it go?" Her voice was breathless.

"How are you, Lexi?"

There was a confused pause. "Uh, fine. But what the hell happened?"

"It's a bit complicated."

"Why?"

"Can you get Amelia's car seat and diaper bag ready?"

"Sure," said Lexi.

Devin tipped the phone beneath her chin, addressing Lucas. "You do have a backseat in that sports car, right?"

His eyes narrowed.

"Lucas is going to pick her up."

Lexi's voice lowered to a growl. "He didn't. Tell me he did not get custody."

"No." Devin kept her voice even. "It's just a visit." She watched Lucas carefully. She'd seen his reaction to Amelia's crying, the fear and loathing of her messy diaper. No way, no how, was the man going to put himself into a position where he was alone with her.

But instead of capitulating, Lucas gave an almost imperceptible shake of his head. He pressed a number on his phone. "Beauchamp Nanny Service?" He held Devin's gaze while he spoke. "I'm going to need a nanny within the hour."

Devin swore under her breath.

"What was that?" asked Lexi.

"I'll be home in an hour," Devin responded.

"The car seat?"

"I'll tell you about it when I get there." Devin ended the call.

"I'll call you right back," Lucas said into his phone. Then he tucked it into his pocket and looked expectantly at Devin. "So, how long will it take you to pack?"

Lucas watched while two members of the household staff lugged the last of Devin and Amelia's belongings up the wide, curving staircase that rose from the octagonal entry foyer of the Demarco mansion. It was completely dark now, and Devin had tartly informed him a few minutes ago that it was past Amelia's bedtime, before pointedly closing the nursery door in his face.

"Told you not to trust him," Byron Phoenix said as he ambled into the two-story foyer from the hallway that led to the great room and the study.

"I never trusted him," Lucas responded, turning to face his deceased mother's second husband, Byron, who was dressed in his usual blue jeans and Western-style shirt. His trimmed brown hair was streaked with silver. He had a highball in his hand—cola and something. His custom-leather tooled boots clicked against the tile floor.

"He shelled out for her lawyers?" Byron came to a halt, his broad shoulders squaring, thumbs hooking into his belt loops while his gaze followed the stairs to the second floor where Devin and Amelia had been given adjoining rooms with a shared bathroom.

"Probably should have seen that one coming," Lucas admitted. At least it explained why Steve had gone out to Lake Westmire, and why Devin had at first denied the fact that he'd been there. "At least she's finally home."

"But so is that mama bear Devin Hartley," Byron pointed out.

"She is a problem," Lucas admitted. He'd won today, but then so had Devin.

Byron puffed out his broad chest. "We shoot intruders back in Texas."

"If we shot intruders here in Seattle, you'd have been dead years ago."

"You know I loved your mama." Byron's words weren't defensive, he was simply stating fact.

It had taken Lucas a few years, but he'd come to respect that the rough Texas cattle baron made his mother—Crystal—happy.

"Back then, everyone called *you* an intruder," Lucas pointed out.

"Are you defending Devin?"

"No." Lucas hadn't meant to take up Devin's side. She was a very big problem for him. She obviously wasn't going to disappear easily, and now she had Steve to bankroll her efforts.

Lucas glanced at Byron's crystal glass and decided a drink was a good idea. He started toward the great room, which was

accessed by a wood-panel and portrait-lined hallway. Byron
fell into step.

"What's your next move?" asked Byron.

Lucas had been thinking about that. "Since she just matched
my biggest advantage over her—legal resources—I suppose I'll
have to match her biggest advantage over me."

"You going to put on a wig and an apron?"

"Funny."

The big man grinned. "I thought so."

"Amelia adores her." Lucas knew he had to make certain
Amelia was comfortable with him, too.

The amused grin grew on Byron's face as they entered the
softly lit room. "Lucas Demarco, Uncle of the Year?"

"How hard can it be?" Lucas paused. "I mean, I'll hire a
nanny for the sticky stuff. But I can read her a book, build her
a castle or play catch or something."

"That little gal can't even walk yet."

"You know what I mean."

Byron turned thoughtful. "You do know that Bernard and
Botlow have had past dealings with Pacific Robotics, right?"

"I'm aware," said Lucas, his gaze going to the bank of picture
windows that looked out over the concrete terrace, the sloping
lawn of the estate and the lights of the ships on Puget Sound
below.

"If you were to ask, the court might just declare that a conflict
of interest."

"Or they might consider me an obstructionist for trying to
block Devin's legal support."

"And give little ol' Devin the sympathy vote," Byron
concluded.

"Sweet young aunt," Lucas mused out loud, a picture of
Devin's fresh, girl-next-door beauty flashing in his mind as
he poured himself two fingers of Macallan. "Self-employed
and making ends meet at a lakeshore cottage in a bucolic little
community with pets and picnic tables. I'm sure she attends
town hall meetings and bakes cookies for good causes. Amelia

clearly adores her. I tell you, the last thing we want to do is turn her into even more of a sympathetic underdog."

"A sympathetic underdog?" It was Devin's surprisingly sharp voice.

Lucas set down the Scotch bottle and turned.

She started across the room, stride confident, shoulders squared. She wore a baggy T-shirt and some kind of clingy slacks topping white running shoes.

"At least you didn't call me pathetic," she challenged.

Byron recovered first and stepped forward, extending his hand. "Byron Phoenix. Pleased to meet you, ma'am."

"Lawyer?" asked Devin, eyes narrowing as she gave him a brief handshake.

Byron scoffed out a laugh. "Extended family."

Devin raised her brows in an obvious question.

"He was married to my mother," Lucas explained.

"You have a stepfather?" Devin was clearly surprised.

Byron chuckled heartily at that one.

"I was twenty-two when they got married. We hardly played catch."

"My mistake," said Devin.

"Could've taught you to rope steers," Byron remarked.

"Care for a drink?" Lucas asked Devin, his manners belatedly kicking in.

"No thank you." She peered through the wall of windows and out into the yard. "And I don't need the sympathy vote. I'm planning to beat you fair and square. Is there someplace out there I can go for a run?"

"Hear that?" Lucas said to Byron. "She's going jogging. The woman appears to be a paragon of all virtues. I suppose you're a vegetarian teetotaler, as well."

Devin shot him a look of disdain. Then she caught him by surprise, snagging the glass out of his hand and downing a healthy swallow. "I'm not a paragon of anything," she told him, handing the glass back to him, voice only slightly wheezy from the straight Scotch.

Byron couldn't seem to stop himself from chuckling. "The

woman definitely has spunk. Too bad there, Lucas. A shrinking wildflower would have made your life a whole lot easier."

"I sleep better when I run," Devin told him. "And since I don't have the luxury of my own bed, and since Amelia is likely to be up at 4:00 a.m., I'd like to take a quick jog around the grounds if that's all right with you."

"One of the housekeepers can get up with Amelia," Lucas offered.

Devin widened her stance and crossed her arms over her chest. "I'm not staffing out my niece."

"I retract my earlier criticism," said Lucas, holding her gaze. "You're not a paragon, you're a purist."

"I'm only trying to survive." For a split second, a flash of unvarnished hurt traced through her eyes.

Lucas felt a shot of empathy. Devin's sister might have broken his brother's heart, and Devin might blame Konrad for Monica's death, but they'd both suffered a terrible loss. They shared that much.

Then she blinked, and the moment was gone, and she was his adversary once more.

He downed the remains of the drink. "I'll show you."

"Show me what?"

"Where you can jog."

"Just point it out. I'll find my way."

But Lucas was already on his way to change. "Meet me on the pool deck. Downstairs, past the kitchen."

Devin didn't know why she'd waited. It wasn't as if she'd get lost on the estate. The extensive yard was well lit, and she was fairly certain it was fenced—not that she was planning to go out of sight of the big mansion anyway. There were lights on all the way up to the third-floor turret. She'd probably be able to spot it for miles.

The clear water sparkled in the outdoor pool, submerged lights illuminating its beautiful blue depths. She couldn't help but admire the tiered decks and the gardens surrounding the pool. The chairs and loungers were padded with burgundy cushions. Both dining tables and occasional tables dotted the seating areas. Sun umbrellas covered many of the dining tables, while tall propane heaters were placed strategically throughout furniture groupings. It was obvious the Demarco family spent a lot of time out here.

Devin couldn't help feeling as though she's wandered into a five-star resort.

"Ready?" Lucas's footfalls sounded on the wooden steps that led from a sundeck to the pool deck. He wore runners, a pair of lightweight black shorts and a sleeveless gray T-shirt with a Seattle Mariners team logo across the front.

"I don't need a babysitter," she informed him, trying valiantly not to notice the definition of his biceps and broad shoulders. Nobody had ever accused the Demarco men of being unattractive. With dark eyes, strong chins and straight aristocratic noses, both Lucas and Konrad often graced the cover of *Seattle Entrepreneur.* The urbane and sexy image was what had attracted Monica to Konrad in the first place.

How could an ordinary woman be expected to resist when one of the Demarco brothers set his sights on her? Predictably, Konrad had swept Monica off her feet. It had taken her about five minutes to fall in love with him. And though she'd later been angry with herself for being duped into doing so, and furious with Konrad for doing the duping, Devin also knew that Monica had never actually fallen out of love with her husband.

"How far do you want to go?" asked Lucas.

Devin wished the question hadn't turned into a double entendre inside her head. She wished even harder that her expression hadn't given her away.

"I meant jogging," said Lucas with a knowing smirk.

"I know what you meant."

"But I'm open to discussion…."

"In your dreams."

"Apparently, in yours."

"Get over yourself. Two miles."

"Is that all?"

She glared at him. "Five, then." It would mean she'd get to

bed later, but it would be worth it to show Lucas she wasn't a wimp.

He shrugged easily. "This way then." He pointed to a bark mulch path that wound down the sloping hill toward Puget Sound. At the same time, he gave a wave to the house behind him. It must have been some kind of a signal, because the path lit up with pot lights in front of them, highlighting an emerald lawn, bushy shrubs and fragrant flower gardens.

Okay, much as she resented the Demarcos, and resented staying here, and resented having to fight for her rights with Amelia, this was one gorgeous estate.

Devin started off slowly, letting her heart rate increase and pump oxygenated blood into her muscles.

Lucas was slightly ahead, so she increased her pace to come abreast. He lengthened his stride to stay in front, and she cursed him under her breath. The showoff.

"What's that?" she asked him, nodding toward a rectangular building, half from curiosity, and half to show him she had enough breath to carry on a conversation.

"A garage," he responded, dropping back to run beside her. "Konrad liked antique cars."

It was an awfully big garage. "Did he have a collection?"

Lucas nodded. "Twenty-five, I think. Oldest is a Model T, right up to a '56 Caddy. A Coupe de Ville, burgundy and cream."

"And over there?" Devin asked, indicating a distant building up the hill with a few lights shining from windows.

"The stables," said Lucas. "You ride?"

Devin shook her head. Horseback riding wasn't something most middle-class urban kids learned growing up.

"Go ahead and try it while you're here."

"I don't plan to be here that long."

He glanced down, the ocean breeze wafting through his short dark hair. "You know something I don't about the court date?"

"I hope they move it up."

"Why?"

The answer was obvious. "So Amelia and I can go home."

His voice went soft in the cool night air. "What if I win?"

She tossed her own short hair, determined to show the man nothing but confidence. "The only thing you've got going for you is money."

"Money helps."

"It also corrupts."

The path curved, and they began a gentle uphill climb. Devin breathed deeply, determined to keep up her pace. She didn't want to show Lucas one iota of weakness, on any front.

"Amelia's got a whole lot of money of her own," he pointed out.

"I assume that's held in trust." Devin didn't want Amelia's money.

"You assume right. For now. But whoever manages her shares in Pacific Robotics will also manage her money. And they had better know what they're doing."

"I can hire a business manager."

"Just like I can hire a nanny."

"You know the obvious solution, don't you?" Devin felt compelled to ask.

"I take guardianship and hire you as a nanny?"

And have Amelia subject to Lucas's whims and control? Not a chance. Devin turned the tables. "I take guardianship and hire you as a business manager."

"Never going to happen." Lucas increased his pace as they passed the horse stables. The boathouse and docks came into view far below at the shore.

Devin struggled to keep up. They were on their way back now, but the mansion was at least a mile away.

She brought herself abreast of him, but he sped up. She did it again, and he went faster still.

Her breathing was becoming erratic, and she'd long since lost any semblance of her regular pace. She was running on adrenaline and frustration, in a futile attempt to keep Lucas from beating her.

"You might want to save your strength," Lucas finally mused. The rat didn't even sound winded.

"I'm fine," she gasped.

He turned around and jogged backward. Even through her humiliation that he could do it so easily, she couldn't help but be grateful that they'd slowed down.

"Don't be stupid, Devin."

She let a glare do her speaking for her.

"This isn't the hill to die on."

"Then why...do you...care who wins?"

He shrugged, allowing a sheepish grin. "It was fun watching you try."

"Rat."

"Guilty." His eyes darkened. "You might want to remember that."

The mansion was closer now. The pool deck a beacon spurring her burning leg muscles forward.

Why, oh, why had she waited for him? She should have set off jogging by herself, done her usual two miles, and been in the shower by now, maybe even in bed, asleep, catching a few precious hours before Amelia woke up, and she started all over again.

Her days were beyond hectic. It had been weeks since she got any decent amount of writing accomplished. Her new self-help book on setting priorities, *Snarled Traffic in the Information Age,* was due to her publisher in three months. And she had eight more chapters to go.

Her feet pounded on the bark mulch.

A hundred yards to go.

Fifty.

Twenty-five.

Thank goodness.

She slowed to a walk, gulping air, keeping well away from Lucas in the hope that he wouldn't see how winded she'd become.

He'd slowed his run, taken it down to a jog, coming to a walk when his feet hit the concrete deck.

Devin took her time joining him, feeling a rush of relief when her lungs slowed back to normal. Her legs were still rubbery, but it was much easier to hide that weakness.

As she approached Lucas, he tossed her a chilled water bottle. She caught it in midair. Obviously someone had set them out while they were away running. What a life the man led.

Devin cracked the seal and took a long, satisfying drink. Her heart rate was getting back to normal, but she knew she'd have some very sore muscles in the morning. She'd give her eyeteeth for a miracle where Amelia slept until seven.

Lucas flopped down on a lounger, gesturing to a low table between it and another identical chair. "Care for some fruit?"

Devin realized she was famished, and the fruit platter looked delicious. The temptation to rest her weary legs was too much to resist. She took the other lounger and stretched out.

Lucas popped a grape into his mouth and munched. "You have everything you need in the nursery?"

Devin selected a slice of pineapple. "It's a dream nursery."

It was.

From the custom-made crib to the designer sheets, to a rocking chair she could practically live in, to a state-of-the-art baby monitor, paintings, mobiles, curtains and the thickest white carpet she'd ever stepped on, Amelia might as well have been a princess.

Devin nibbled the edge of the pineapple. "You must have been pretty confident you'd need it."

"I was." He turned his head to watch her. "I am." He paused. "You should really give up now."

"Sure." She shrugged. "Why not. Who needs the grief, anyway? All those lawyers, a court date, fighting you—and you're clearly a superior human being. I might as well just call it quits." She popped the rest of the pineapple into her mouth.

He grinned, and plunked his head back on the lounger, closing his eyes. "Ah, Devin. You're entertaining. I'll give you that much."

She sucked the pineapple juice from her fingertips and tried to stay angry with Lucas. It seemed like too much of an effort. "Okay if we use the pool tomorrow?"

Living on a lakeshore, Devin had already decided to get Amelia accustomed to the water as early as possible. She might as well make the best of being a prisoner at the Demarcos.

"Do anything you want," Lucas answered without opening his eyes. "I'll make sure the staff all know who you are. The cooks will help you with breakfast, or you can feel free to make whatever you want. Give them a list of foods for Amelia, or yourself for that matter. Try out the horses, take out a boat, swim, play tennis—"

"Amelia's a little young for tennis."

"I meant you. There's an army of people here who can babysit."

"Teresa is listening to the baby monitor right now," Devin said.

It felt supremely self-indulgent to take advantage of the Demarco staff, but without Lexi next door, Devin knew she'd need at least occasional help. Hopefully, the times would be few and far between. She'd needed to tire herself out before bed tonight, but she certainly wouldn't be abandoning Amelia to take tennis lessons.

"I'd like to spend some time with Amelia," said Lucas.

His statement caught Devin's attention. "Why?"

Lucas opened his eyes and turned. "She's my niece."

"You're afraid of her."

"I am not," he denied. "Okay, I'm a little afraid of the slimy bits."

Devin fought a smirk. "The slimy bits are what make her a baby."

"I prefer clean, dry babies."

"Those are called adults."

Lucas frowned. "I want her to get to know me."

"I know. So I won't have an advantage over you in court." She shook her head and gave a dry chuckle. "She's not a puppy, Lucas. We're not going to put her down between us and see who she runs to."

Lucas's eyes hardened, but he didn't answer.

She helped herself to a slice of kiwi. "But how very Machiavellian of you to think that way."

"She's Konrad's daughter." All traces of humor and friendliness were gone from his voice.

"And a ten-percent shareholder of Pacific Robotics. I understand completely."

His jaw tightened, and a muscle ticked next to his eye. "You haven't a clue."

Oh, but she did.

While he might occasionally appear to let his guard down, Lucas was single-minded in his objective. And that objective was Amelia. And Devin was the only protection the little girl had.

Three

Amelia kicked her tiny feet and gurgled happily in the Demarcos' pool the following afternoon. She looked darling in a red-and-white striped bathing suit, and she'd taken immediately to splashing and ducking.

"I may have a solution," said Lexi on a happy sigh from where she was bobbing around in the deep end on a yellow air mattress. She wore a turquoise one-piece that accented her healthy body. Lexi wasn't one to exercise, but she was on the go so much that she stayed in great shape. A pair of big sunglasses covered her eyes.

"What's your solution?" Devin asked, smiling as she blew a puff of air into Amelia's face. The baby sucked in a breath and scrunched her eyes shut, then Devin gently ducked her underwater.

"Lucas can adopt me instead."

"What a great idea," Devin singsonged as she lifted Amelia back out of the water.

The baby squealed and kicked in delight, nearly wiggling out of Devin's grasp.

"A win for you," said Lexi. "A win for me."

"Not so much for me," Lucas said in a dry voice.

Lexi popped her sunglasses up onto her head to squint at Lucas where he stood on the deck, while Devin turned in the pool so that she faced him. He should have looked out of place in his business suit, feet braced apart, tie neatly knotted at his throat. But for some reason, the outfit made Devin self-conscious of her aqua-colored bikini instead.

Lexi didn't miss a beat. "I don't see why not. I don't throw temper tantrums, and I'm fully potty-trained."

"I can vouch for that," said Devin.

Lucas shook his head, apparently unamused. "I'll be out for an hour or so. Do you need anything?"

"We're fine," said Devin, keeping her attention on Amelia, wishing she didn't find Lucas so attractive. She had absolutely no business thinking about him as anything other than an enemy.

She could feel Lucas's gaze on her for a long moment. Then she heard him turn away, and she dared to look up as he took the staircase to the concrete pathway, walked past the garden, below the sprawling oak tree, and disappeared into the mansion.

"He's even better looking than Konrad." Lexi sighed.

"You think?" asked Devin, taking Amelia's chubby hands in hers and drawing the baby forward in a front float.

"Don't pretend you didn't notice," Lexi admonished, lying back and stroking a hand through the water, recentering herself in the deep end of the pool.

"I didn't notice," Devin lied. "I was too busy fighting him in court."

"Doesn't mean you can't look."

"It means there's absolutely *nothing* about the man that I like."

"I liked his ass," teased Lexi.

"Then *you* are a cougar."

"And I am sorely disappointed to hear that," came a drawling voice, a clear thread of amusement running through it.

Devin glanced up to see Byron, arms crossed over his chest, feet planted firmly apart, staring openly at Lexi while she sunbathed. He wore faded blue jeans, a denim shirt with the sleeves rolled up and a pair of brown cowboy boots.

"Eyes front, old man," said Lexi with a waggle of her finger. "I'm not here for your visual entertainment."

Byron didn't look away.

Devin lifted Amelia from the water and cradled her cool body against her chest. "Byron, this is my friend Lexi. Lexi, Byron is Lucas's…what do I call you? Widowed stepfather?"

"I'd say we can go with 'friend'," Byron responded, still staring openly at Lexi where she lay on the air mattress.

Lexi pushed her sunglasses back up to the top of her head and propped herself on one elbow. "Do you have a reason for being here?"

Devin coughed out a laugh at Lexi's blunt manner.

"I believe I do." He turned his attention to Devin. "I was hoping to have a little talk with you, young lady."

Devin hesitated, not really anxious to be grilled by Byron. "About…?" she asked.

"Come on up here, and I'll tell you all about it."

Devin stayed put.

"I'm not gonna bite you," he assured her with a grin.

She glanced down at Amelia and saw that the tiny girl was worn out. They were going to have to get out of the water soon anyway. And she had a feeling Byron would wait.

"Why not?" she muttered. The man clearly had something to say. She might as well get this over with. She made her way toward the wide staircase at the end of the pool.

She took a butter-yellow towel from the rack at the edge of the pool deck and wrapped it around Amelia to keep her from getting chilled.

Byron watched her approach. Then he gestured to a lounge chair. Devin accepted his offer, stretching out her legs, draping the ends of the big towel across her bare stomach and thighs.

The sun was warm on her wet limbs and her rapidly drying hair.

As Byron sat down in the lounger on the other side of a small square table, his glance flicked critically to Lexi. Devin didn't offer to ask Lexi to leave. Whatever the man had to say, he could say in front of her friend.

Byron seemed to accept the situation. "I hear tell you've met Steve Foster."

"I have." She focused her attention on adjusting the towel, making sure Amelia's pale, delicate skin was protected from the sun.

After a moment, she looked back up into the silence to see Byron regarding her with penetrating hazel eyes and a grim line of a mouth.

"You know there's been some trouble between those boys."

Devin gave a small shrug. "Steve's helping me out. Lucas is fighting against me. Is that the trouble you're talking about?"

Water sloshed in the pool as Lexi came off the air mattress.

"More to it than that," Byron corrected.

Devin steadfastly met his gaze. "Anything else is none of my business."

"I'd be willin' to bet that it is."

She shook her head in denial as Lexi made her way through the shallow end and out of the pool.

"You're the latest pawn in a feud that goes back a considerable long time."

"I'm not going to be anybody's pawn." Devin couldn't care less about the emotional and financial entanglements of the Demarco family. She was fighting for Amelia, and that was the end of it.

"What is it you've got in mind for an endgame?"

Devin didn't understand.

Lexi wrapped a towel, sarong-style, around her dripping wet body and slicked back her blond hair as she moved toward them.

Byron's gaze tracked Lexi until she sat down. Then he glanced back to Devin. "What is it you're hoping to get out of this?"

"Amelia," Devin answered.

Byron's skepticism came through in his squint. He leaned forward. "Just between you, me and the hitching post?"

Devin leaned toward him. "Amelia," she repeated.

There was a long pause.

"And you think ol' Steve can give you a hand with that."

"We think he's the only one who's offered," said Lexi, from the lounger next to Devin.

Byron stared first at Lexi and then at Devin. "And why do you supposed he's offered to help?"

Devin kept her voice low since Amelia was drifting off to sleep. "I don't particularly care."

Steve's lawyers were giving her a fighting chance against Lucas.

"Altruism?" Byron mocked.

"A concept you're obviously unfamiliar with," Lexi retorted.

Byron ignored Lexi and spoke directly to Devin. "He's sidling up to you like some slick ol' polecat. He helps you now. You help him later. If you know what I mean."

Devin blinked. "Have I done something to make you think I'm stupid?"

Byron drew back in obvious surprise.

"I'm taking Steve's offer at face value. I haven't made him a single promise."

In fact, she'd offered an outright deal to Lucas to manage the shares if he'd let her keep Amelia, but he didn't trust her enough to agree.

And who was to say Steve was the bad guy in this little family drama anyway? So far, she'd put the black hat firmly on Lucas's head. He was the one who'd plotted with Konrad to trick Monica and produce an heir to their grandfather's company shares. Devin hadn't forgotten that.

"Steve would steal your last dollar as soon as look at you," Byron warned.

"As opposed to Lucas?" she asked.

"Lucas lets you see him coming."

Devin gave a nod to that. Lucas had certainly been up front about the fact that he wanted to take Amelia away from her. He'd also been pretty clear that his interest in the baby was financial.

Devin found her hold tightening on Amelia.

"Listen up," said Byron, shifting in the lounger so he faced Devin more directly.

"No, you listen *up*," Lexi interrupted. "You are not going to convince Devin to give up her lawyers."

"I had no intention—"

"Of course you did. That's what this whole pretty, 'don't trust the evil Steve' speech was leading up to. And it's not going to work."

"I'm simply suggesting she might want to be careful."

Lexi crossed her arms over her chest. With a glance at Amelia's sleeping form, she lowered her voice. "We *are* being careful." She paused. "We don't trust anyone...including you."

Devin agreed with Lexi on that point. There wasn't a single member of the Demarco family she could afford to trust. She was on her own in this. Well, except for Lexi.

Byron heaved a large sigh. "I guess there's nothing left for me to say."

"No," Lexi agreed. "There's not."

Byron glanced back to Devin. "I'm on your side."

She coughed out a laugh of disbelief. "You're on Lucas's side."

"Lucas is an honorable man."

"An honorable man wouldn't try to rip an innocent baby from the arms of her loving aunt."

Byron's gaze moved briefly to the sleeping Amelia and then back to Devin. "You're here, aren't you?"

"It was his Hail Mary play in court," she responded. "He only made the offer because he knew the judge was about to rule for me."

Byron came to his feet. He gave his head a small shake, making a clicking sound in his cheek that transmitted his disagreement with her statement. "You can't trust Steve," he said simply.

"Funny," Lexi responded. "That's exactly what Steve says about the rest of you."

* * *

"You cannot leave Amelia with these people," Lexi stage-whispered after Byron had disappeared into the house.

"No kidding," Devin responded.

She poured herself a glass of iced tea from a pitcher that someone had placed on the table. Devin felt a twinge of guilt for letting herself be waited on by the Demarco staff. But she was thirsty, and she didn't want to disturb Amelia.

Lexi followed suit. "Why can't rich people be nice?" she asked as the ice cubes clinked against her glass. "If I was rich, I'd still be nice."

"That should be my new book proposal," Devin mused, getting another twinge of guilt when she talked about writing. She was behind on her manuscript, and her deadline was looming. *"Nice and Rich,"* she said, trying a title on for size. *"The Art of Doing Them Both Together."* It actually wasn't half-bad.

Lexi lifted her glass in a mock toast. "The rich truly do need your help."

Devin grimaced. "Unfortunately, I don't know the first thing about being rich."

"Take a look at all this," said Lexi, gesturing in a circle. "What better place to do your research?"

Devin rolled the idea around in her head.

She glanced from the pool to the tennis courts, the private dock and boathouse, and the humongous mansion that required a map to navigate. It didn't get much richer than this. And the Demarcos were certainly prime examples of nasty.

Her editor would probably be a lot more forgiving of a late manuscript if she had another book idea in the hopper.

"Here he comes again," Lexi intoned.

"Byron?" Devin resisted the urge to twist her head to see the staircase behind her.

"Lucas." Lexi took a sip of the iced tea, leaned back and adjusted the damp towel. "You might want to start taking notes."

Devin couldn't help a calculating smirk as Lucas made his

way across the pool deck. She wondered how he'd feel about starring in her next book.

He was still wearing his business suit and a pair of perfectly shined dress shoes, though it had to be seventy degrees this afternoon, hotter in the sunshine. His glance went to Amelia, and he seemed to realize she was sleeping.

"I need to talk to you," he whispered.

"You can use your normal voice," Devin responded, finding herself watching him closely, thinking about his life and his world and how she might use the Demarcos as fodder for her next book. "Just don't shout."

"Okay," he agreed, testing the chair that Byron had vacated earlier with the back of his hand. Apparently, satisfied that it was dry, he sat down sideways, those expensively shod feet firmly planted on the textured, concrete deck.

He gazed at Amelia for a long minute. Then he glanced to Devin, uncertainty plain on his aristocratic face. "I can...uh, hold her. That is, if you don't mind."

Devin's mouth quirked in a reflexive grin. "You want to hold Amelia?"

He smoothed his palms along his suit pants. "Yes. Sure." He nodded, still watching Amelia as if he was afraid she might explode. "I'd like to hold her."

"Why?"

His gray eyes narrowed. "Because she's my niece."

Devin shifted a little, but Amelia didn't stir. It was probably a good time for Lucas to take another shot. "Have you ever held a baby before?"

"Just the one time," he admitted.

Devin couldn't help but note the wary expression on his face. "Okay." She scooted carefully forward.

At the last minute, she realized that once Amelia was out of her arms, she'd be sitting here in nothing but her bikini. She gritted her teeth and told herself to buck up. Lucas would probably be so busy worrying about Amelia that he wouldn't even notice.

She rose and placed the baby carefully in his arms.

His gaze shifted to her cleavage and stayed there.

She quickly straightened and stepped back. She briefly debated dashing across the deck to get herself another towel, but she decided that would be too obvious.

She sat down on the lounger and laid back, pretending she didn't care about the bikini and truly appreciating the empty arms. She enjoyed holding Amelia, but the baby girl did get heavy after a while.

Lexi had kept silent, watching with undisguised interest while Lucas held Amelia.

He seemed to relax ever so slightly, turning, shifting back and putting his legs up on the lounger. He gingerly moved Amelia to a more comfortable position. She wriggled in the big towel, but then went still.

Devin tried not to notice how good he looked with a baby in his arms. For some reason, the bundle of sleeping Amelia seemed to soften the edges of his expression. He came across as protective instead of harsh. It made him even more attractive, if that was possible.

"What did you want to talk about?" she asked him, hoping he wasn't round two of a tag-team match with Byron.

"A nanny," said Lucas, his attention still fixed on Amelia.

"There's no rush," she responded. "I'm perfectly capable of taking care of Amelia."

"I know you are," he acknowledged. "But you might not always be here."

She glared at him.

"Is that a threat?" Lexi asked.

Lucas seemed to remember she was there. "I've never made a secret of the fact that I intend to win guardianship," he told them both.

"As do I," said Devin.

Lucas stared evenly back at her. "If you do, you can fire the nanny. If not, I thought you might like to help me choose." He paused, while Devin sorted the offer out in her mind.

She didn't want to even consider the possibility of leaving Amelia with Lucas. Her brain almost refused to go to the worst-case scenario. But it might come to that. And if it did, and she had to leave... Her stomach contracted with pain, and she had to resist the urge to snatch Amelia out of Lucas's arms.

If it came to that, wouldn't she feel better knowing who was caring for Amelia? And would it not be in her best interest to develop a positive relationship with her?

"I'm not a monster," said Lucas.

Lexi gave a grunt of disbelief.

Lucas shot her a quelling look before returning his attention to Devin. "I'm after exactly the same thing as you."

"For very different reasons."

He shook his head and sighed. "I'm going to choose a nanny, Devin. You can help me or not, it's entirely up to—" He gasped in horror.

Devin sat bolt upright in shock. "What?"

Lucas nearly leveled her with a look. "Is this child wearing a diaper?"

Devin shouldn't laugh. She *couldn't* laugh. Oh, dear. She quickly clapped her hand to her mouth.

"I am wearing a Brioni suit," Lucas ground from between clenched teeth.

"Sorry about that," Devin managed to say.

"You might have mentioned—"

"I forgot," she answered honestly.

"Forgive me if I have a hard time believing you."

"I didn't mean..." But she was struggling once more not to laugh. "Babies *are* messy," she warned him.

"Is this your idea of revenge?"

"It's my idea of letting you be an uncle. They pee, Lucas. They also drool and spit up. And they even—"

"I've already experienced *that*," he growled.

"Be a man about it," Lexi said.

"It's a six-thousand-dollar suit," he barked at her.

Amelia opened her eyes, took one look at Lucas and howled in fear.

He stiffened at the sound. "Oh, for the love of..."

Devin popped up out of the lounger and rescued Amelia.

Lucas's shirt, slacks and the lower part of his jacket were dark with wetness.

He stared down at his lap. "There is a reason they invented diapers," he intoned.

"Accidents do happen," said Devin, cradling the damp, but rapidly calming Amelia against her chest.

Lucas's glare told her he considered this anything but.

"Nannies," said Lucas, smacking a stack of résumés down next to Devin where she sat near one end of the long dining-room table, her laptop open in front of her. After this afternoon's debacle, he realized more than ever that they needed to get themselves organized.

Dinner had long since been cleared away. He assumed Amelia was asleep. And Devin had a cup of tea cooling beside her computer as she typed. A plate of cookies and small pastries was in the middle of the table in front of her, but it didn't look like she'd indulged.

"Accidents do happen," she repeated, obviously correctly identifying the source of his displeasure. She hit another key then closed the laptop.

"Accidents," he responded as he settled into the chair at the end of the table, around the corner from hers, "can be prevented."

"Are you always this controlling?" she asked, glancing at the top nanny résumé.

"I'm always this organized." He lifted the résumé and began reading. "Graduated from the London Royal Nanny Academy in 1978."

"Too old."

He looked up. "I requested someone with experience."

Devin shook her head. "Not that much experience. Amelia will be walking soon, and toddlers are energetic."

"We're looking for a nanny, not a playmate."

Devin set her cup firmly down into the saucer. "*I* expect a good nanny to spend plenty of time playing with Amelia."

"And *I* expect a good nanny to know her way around a changing table."

"You need to get over that, Lucas."

"I am over it." He pointedly went back to reading.

"Sure you are," Devin muttered.

Well, he could be forgiven his frustration. Amelia had looked fairly sweet and harmless while she slept on Devin's lap. It had seemed like a perfect chance for him to stick his toe in the water of uncle-hood. How was he to know the baby was effectively booby-trapped?

But Devin had known.

He strongly suspected she'd set him up. But it would take more than that to dissuade him from bonding with Amelia. He'd already started reading a couple of how-to books. He'd master baby-raising or die trying.

He refocused his attention on the résumé in front of him. "It says she's orderly, organized and—within her standard routine template—will customize a schedule that fits our lifestyle."

"Standard routine template?" Devin's tone was incredulous.

He glanced at her again. "What?"

"There's no standard routine template for raising babies. All babies are unique."

"I'm sure she means meals and naps and walks and things."

"Babies should sleep when they're tired and eat when they're hungry."

Lucas blinked. That sounded an awful lot like chaos to him. "Are you joking?"

"Absolutely not. Routines ought to be child-led for the first few years."

He paused, squinting at her. "You're messing with me, right?"

She whisked the résumé out of his hand and put it facedown on the table. "Next."

"Put the *baby* in charge? Good grief, Devin. It's a baby."

She took the next résumé from the pile. "Early childhood certificate from Boise College."

"Idaho?"

"'Within broad boundaries, will create a positive, nurturing environment that respects the individuality and creativity of each child.'"

"Is that code for raising spoiled, ill-mannered hooligans?"

"I think it's code for kindness and compassion."

Lucas snagged the résumé from her hand and put it facedown with the other. "Next."

"Hey!"

"You get a veto? Then so do I."

Devin compressed her lips.

"You want to split the pile?" he asked. Maybe they could narrow it down a little by swapping their acceptable choices.

"Can we do it tomorrow?"

Lucas glanced at his watch. Nine-thirty. "What's wrong with now?" He didn't believe in procrastination. When a job needed to get done, you did it.

"I'm a little tired."

He couldn't help a reflexive eye-roll. "From swimming in the pool and lounging in the sun?"

She retrieved the laptop case from the chair beside her and slid open the zipper. "Those iced-tea glasses were *awfully* heavy."

Her joke caught him off guard. He'd expected a snappy, if not angry retort to his jab.

"I'd like to get this over with," he explained.

"Look." She sighed. "It may seem early to you, but I've had approximately six hours sleep a night, in two or three separate segments, for the past three months. I'm tired." She gestured to the laptop. "I have a deadline. I'd like to take a quick run, have a quick bath and try my best to rejuvenate my brain cells before Amelia wakes up again."

Devin stuffed the laptop inside the case, zipped it up and came to her feet. He stood with her. The light from the chandelier caught her face, and for the first time he noticed dark circles under her eyes.

Up until now, he'd been distracted by the sapphire-blue of her irises. They glowed when she smiled at Amelia, flared when she was angry and turned crystal clear when her brain was working on a problem or coming up with a clever retort to something he'd said.

Right now, they seemed faded, like a misty sky on a southern summer day.

"You okay?" he automatically asked.

She tipped her head, gazing up at him. "I'm fine. Just tired."

"You sure you want to run?" He thought about offering to accompany her again. But he'd been a bit of a cad last time. He wasn't exactly sure what he was trying to prove. The fact that he had longer, more muscular legs perhaps?

"I'm sure," she answered.

"You know," he couldn't help but point out, "the sooner we find a nanny, the sooner you can get some more sleep."

She closed her eyes for a split second, her shoulders seeming to droop. He had to check the urge to reach out and steady her.

"I was wrong when I said you were controlling," she told him.

Progress? He felt hope rise.

"You're not controlling. You are excruciatingly goal-oriented."

She made it sound like a flaw.

"It only comes across as controlling," she continued, "because you try to drag the rest of the world along with you."

"Sometimes the world needs a little dragging."

Take Devin. She could get an extra hour of sleep tonight, or she could agree with him on a nanny and get extra sleep from here on in. It was a no-brainer to Lucas.

"Sometimes you have to stop and smell the roses," she told him.

"They don't bloom until July," he pointed out.

Devin cracked a small smile at that, even as she shook her head. Then she reached for her laptop case, and Lucas automatically reached out to lift it for her, brushing her shoulder with his forearm as he leaned around her.

The touch was electric, and he reflexively jerked away. The action brought the front of his thigh against the side of hers, and sexual energy jump-started his body.

What was the matter with him?

Sure, she was a gorgeous woman. But he'd been careful to keep that in perspective. He had no call, no business, no *right* to think of her as anything other than an obstruction. He wanted Amelia, and Devin was in his way. Wanting Devin was nowhere in the plan.

He sucked in a breath, lifting her laptop, drawing away. Wanting Devin? No way. Not going there. Not ever.

Devin followed on Lucas's heels as he carried her laptop along the wide hallway on the main floor of the mansion. Her shoulder and thigh still buzzed from their contact. Was that really the first time he'd touched her? Ever?

She searched her brain, but she couldn't remember another occasion. And apparently, the experience would have been seared into her spinal column.

"You can use this one as an office," he was saying as they neared the front foyer. He opened a door off the hall, revealing a small library.

He hit the light switch, and a desk lamp came on, bathing the room in a soft glow.

The library's walls were lined with ornate wooden shelves and what looked like an eclectic selection of books. There was a rosewood desk, a patterned area rug and two cream-colored wingback chairs with ottomans that complemented a compact leather chair positioned behind the desk. The room was surprisingly feminine, with touches of pattern china and figurines placed beside the books, and the occasional watercolor seascape recessed into the shelves.

"My mother used to like this room," said Lucas.

"Are you sure you want me to use it?" She'd been complaining about her deadline to make a point, and to have an excuse to go to bed. She hadn't intended for Lucas to try to solve her problem.

"Yes. Of course." He set her laptop on the desk and turned to face her where she stood a few steps into the room. "You need somewhere quiet to concentrate."

"Once Amelia is asleep—"

He leaned back against the desk, bracing his hands on either side. "You said you had a deadline."

"I do."

"Then you'll let the nanny monitor Amelia, and you will—"

"Are you trying to keep me away from Amelia?"

His brows went up in obvious shock. "No," he answered simply.

She was inclined to believe him, and she felt her guard go down a notch.

"Then, what are you doing?" she asked. Why did he care about her deadline?

"I'm offering you a place to work."

She studied his expression, the tight mouth, cool slate eyes, dark imposing brow. "You're being nice to me," she accused.

"So?"

"So, it's out of character. So, I'm trying to figure out what you're up to."

"I'm not a monster, Devin."

The sound of her name made her chest go tight. "But you are rather cold-blooded."

Silence followed her words.

Then he straightened away from the desk. He took a step toward her, then another, and another. A glow of awareness crept into his eyes. "Devin," he whispered. "At the moment, I am not feeling even remotely cold-blooded."

She tipped her chin to look at him. For the life of her, she couldn't come up with a retort.

He smelled fresh as a sea breeze. His skin was shaved close, his hair neatly trimmed and his gray eyes flecked with silver. His softened lips captured her undivided attention.

"What are you doing?" she managed to rasp. She ordered her legs to move, to leave, to flee, but they didn't obey.

"I wish I knew."

His index finger touched the bottom of her chin. His breath puffed, soft and sweet, as his head tilted sideways.

"We can't," she murmured.

There was absolutely no doubting his intentions. But she found herself subconsciously stretching up. Her skin flushed hot. Her eyes fluttered closed. Then his lips brushed hers.

His arm snaked around the small of her back, tugging her to him, pulling her flat against his chest.

He swooped down and kissed her deeply. Her body instantly responded. Her arms wound around his neck. Her head tipped sideways. Her lips parted, tongue tangling.

An eternity later, as the blood pounded through her brain and arousal peaked across every inch of her body, Lucas suddenly broke the kiss. His breathing was loud, and she could swear she heard his heartbeat matching her own.

"Turns out," he gasped, clasping her upper arms firmly and putting some space between them, "we can."

Embarrassment washed over her.

She bit down on the heat of her lower lip and finger-combed her short hair back into submission, mortified that she let him kiss her, that she'd kissed him back, enthusiastically.

It would have been bad enough if she hadn't liked it. But oh, dear, she had really, really liked it. She struggled to bring her hormones back into submission.

Like she had while they were jogging, she was completely off her pace, out of control. Her world was spinning wildly around her, and there was nothing she could do to stop it.

"That was bad," she told him, shaking her head. "That was stupid. We are *not* going to let this happen again."

They absolutely could not go around falling into each other's arms, kissing each other, getting lost in passion when there were serious issues between them.

It was important they came to an agreement on that.

He didn't respond.

"Lucas," she prompted.

His eyes focused on her. "What? You want me to lie?"

Four

Devin had escaped the Demarco mansion first thing the next morning, taking Amelia in her car and heading to Lake Westmire, well away from any possibility of a chance encounter with Lucas. She decided she would check on her plants, pack a few more of Amelia's clothes, listen to any messages on her answering machine and double-check the fridge for anything that might spoil during the few weeks she'd be away.

Lexi stopped by the house during Amelia's afternoon nap. She convinced Devin to join her for a catamaran ride across the bay once the baby woke up. Devin was happy with the excuse to extend her visit. She decided that after the sail, she'd give Amelia her dinner, freshen her up in a bath and then let her fall asleep on the way back to the Demarco mansion.

Out on the lake, in her little swimsuit and a cotton cover-up, Amelia sat happily between Devin's legs, bouncing on the catamaran's trampoline deck. When the cool water splashed up through the springy, open-knit fabric, she grabbed at it with her hands, giggling when it disappeared from her little fingers.

"Define kiss," said Lexi, adjusting the main sail with practiced maneuvers as she changed their direction and they skimmed out across the rippling water.

"A regular kiss," said Devin.

"On the lips."

"Yes." Devin wasn't sure anything else would have been

noteworthy. Though she supposed Lucas kissing her on the cheek or forehead would have been pretty weird, too.

"Full frontal hugging?" asked Lexi.

"Yes," Devin admitted. And, wow, that had been one great hug.

"Groping?"

"No," she quickly denied.

"But the kiss was good?" Lexi persisted.

"The kiss was great," Devin confirmed on a huge sigh of frustration. It would probably go down in the record books as one of her all-time favorite kisses. Whatever his ethics, whatever his conduct, Lucas Demarco knew how to kiss a woman.

She compulsively rolled one of the webbing straps on Amelia's life jacket into a tight spiral, then she let it spring back open in her hand. "But I don't get why he did it." The question had plagued her all night long.

"Sometimes guys don't have a reason," Lexi offered, swooping some loose strands of hair back from her face as the wind grew stronger. "They take random action. And, when it comes to sex, they're ruled by their primal brains."

"Number one, it wasn't sex. And number two, Lucas is not a random guy." And Devin doubted his primal brain ruled any of his actions. "He's logical, organized and compulsively goal-oriented. When he does something, it's for a reason."

"Do you really think you need to add paranoia to this situation?" Lexi pushed hard on the tiller.

The boat canted to one side, and Devin braced herself with a rope handle, holding tight to Amelia. "It doesn't count as paranoia, when they truly are out to get you."

Lexi rocked her head back and forth, obviously considering the merits of Devin's point.

"I've been thinking," Devin added, completely convinced that Lucas's kiss was part of some well thought out, detailed plan to gain an advantage over her. "I'm not going to just sit back and wait for his next move."

She anchored her white baseball cap on her head. "If all I do is react to his maneuvers, then I'm going to lose. That's what happened in the temporary guardianship hearing. He had a plan. I didn't. And it cost me."

Lexi loosened the sail. "So, what are you going to do?"

"Make a plan," Devin answered logically.

"No kidding, Sherlock. What kind of a plan?"

"I'm going to need your help with that."

It needed to be devious, brilliant, but the simpler the better. It needed to paint Lucas into a corner, but he couldn't see it coming.

"You could kiss him again," Lexi offered.

"That's the best you can do?"

"You'd turn the tables on him. You're a gorgeous woman, you know."

Devin could see where Lexi was going with this. But is wasn't something she'd be able to pull off. "I'm not exactly a vamp."

Lexi's voice was laced with laughter. "But you could be. You glam up good. I'll lend you a dress. We'll do your makeup, get you some sleep-with-me heels, mess around with your hair."

Devin chuckled in return. "And then what?"

"And then he's putty in your hands."

"And…?"

"A little pillow talk. You learn his secrets."

Devin splashed some water at Lexi. "I'm not going to sleep with him."

"Of course not. Just, you know, put on some sexy clothes, give him a couple of come-hither looks. If you can learn something useful about Konrad—or about Lucas for that matter—you can take it to court."

Lexi leaned far back to balance the boat in a freshening wind. Devin tightened her hold on Amelia and shifted her weight to help out. The sail rippled loudly in the wind.

"It might work," Devin called to Lexi. "I find concrete proof that Lucas and Konrad plotted Amelia's birth for their own financial ends, and I'm home free."

Lexi slowed the boat down as they neared her beach. "And if he's already playing you on the sexual front?"

"Then I'll lull him into a false sense of security." Devin

wasn't scared. Okay, she was a little intimidated at the thought of playing sexual politics with Lucas. But it was for a good cause, and she'd simply have to make sure she kept her wits about her.

Lexi turned the boat for home. "You should also snoop through his house."

"I've been thinking about talking to the staff," said Devin. "Just idle chitchat. I'm not going to grill them or anything. And, hey, if there's something interesting lying out there in plain sight…"

Lexi shot her a conspiratorial grin.

"I refuse to sit back and do nothing," Devin defended.

"You have my complete support," said Lexi. "Besides, he's the one who forced you to stay there in the first place."

Devin gave a vigorous nod of agreement. "If he's not smart enough to hide the evidence, then he deserves to get caught."

"What do you think you'll find?"

"I have no idea."

"Looks like we've got company." Lexi nodded to the beach in front of their houses.

"Not Lucas." Despite her bold words, Devin wasn't anywhere near ready to put her plan into action. She certainly wasn't ready to face him yet.

After their kiss last night, she'd escaped directly from the library to her room. Then she'd deliberately waited until his sports car pulled out of the driveway this morning before venturing down from the nursery to feed Amelia breakfast. They'd made a clean break. And, if she was lucky, it would last until tomorrow morning.

"It's Steve," said Lexi, adjusting the angle of the catamaran so that it pointed directly at the beach.

As they approached the shore, Devin prepared to jump off. She settled Amelia firmly against one hip, then she turned her body, feet dangling just above the water line.

She jumped and hit the sandy bottom. It slipped away beneath her heels, but she maintained her balance, trotting the last few feet alongside the boat.

She grasped the bow line with one hand, holding Amelia fast with the other. She needn't have worried. Lexi had put the boat expertly up on the beach and quickly jumped off herself.

Steve stood at the water's edge, and he stepped forward and smoothly relieved Devin of Amelia.

"Looked like fun out there," he commented. He held Amelia aloft for a minute, grinning at her and babbling nonsense.

The baby smiled back, cooing a few sounds of her own and reaching for his nose. Steve propped her, bulky life jacket and all, against his shoulder, and Devin couldn't help contrasting his easy manner with the baby against Lucas's awkwardness.

Lexi stripped off her life jacket and started work on the ropes.

"I thought you might need some help," Steve explained to Devin.

Devin stripped off her own life jacket then took Amelia from Steve's arms and unzipped hers. "Help with what?"

"I assumed you were picking up a few more things from the house. For the baby. Maybe for you."

"How did you know I was here?" It was disconcerting to have him show up out of nowhere.

"He pumped the staff for information," came Lucas's unexpected voice.

Devin looked up in surprise to see Lucas striding across the beach, his shoes off, slacks rolled up a few turns and his suit jacket slung over his arm. "He's been spying on you," Lucas told Devin.

"What about you?" Steve challenged.

"They're my staff," Lucas returned.

"Did you two come together?" asked Devin. She wasn't crazy about having any of the Demarco family invading her home turf. It wouldn't be much of a sanctuary if her problems kept following her out here.

"No," they both answered simultaneously.

"Well, I don't need help moving," she said, finishing the exchange with Steve.

Then she turned on Lucas. "And you. There's no reason for you to be here, either."

"I wanted to make sure you were coming back." There was a wealth of awareness in his flat, frank stare. He knew the kiss had disconcerted her. And he'd obviously guessed that's why she had fled.

Well, he was in for a surprise now. She was over the kiss, and she was going to ignore any lingering attraction she might have for him. From now on, he was the target of her investigation, nothing more.

"Of course I'm coming back," she told him breezily, switching her attention on Amelia, fixing her little sun cap and smoothing her wispy hair.

Despite her concentration, she could feel Lucas's gaze. But she assured herself that he didn't know what was going on inside her head. As far as he was concerned, their kiss had meant nothing.

"You should have told me where you were going." There was a rebuke in his voice.

"I'm a prisoner now?" she couldn't help but ask.

"You're under a court order."

She turned to peer at his expression, an unsettling thought taking hold. Would he somehow use this against her? Had he reported her for taking Amelia out of the Demarco mansion?

She advanced on him, voice going low. "What did you do?"

"Damn it!" Lexi shouted from behind her, and Lucas instantly sprang to action.

Devin whirled to see him drop his suit jacket and race into the lake after the catamaran. The wind had picked up, and the craft had slipped from the sand. The breeze caught the mainsail, and the boat was heading out into the middle of the water.

Lexi was chasing it, too, but Lucas was faster. As the water reached his waist, he dove in, swimming powerfully across the waves, only just managing to grab a stern line and hang on tight.

Lexi was chest deep in the water. Steve was still on shore.

And all three of them held their breath while Lucas made his way, hand over hand, along the rope. He grasped a handle on the pontoon and hauled himself, dripping wet, onto the accelerating boat.

"I can't believe he caught it," Lexi breathed. "That was just plain stupid," she cursed herself, her expression telling Devin she'd been needlessly distracted.

"Must have been a sudden gust," Devin offered in consolation, shading her eyes to watch as Lucas took control of the catamaran, ducking under the boom while he tacked to turn.

"Does he know how to sail?" Lexi asked Steve.

Steve nodded, but his lips were drawn in a grim line. There was a chill in his brown eyes that Devin hadn't seen before.

She shifted Amelia and focused on Lucas as he maneuvered in a big arc against the setting sun. Once turned, he lined up, pointing the craft toward them, coming in at a fast clip as he ran the boat back up on the soft sand. Lexi quickly grabbed one of the pontoons. Lucas hopped off and grabbed the other. Together they dragged it a safe distance onto the beach.

Lexi immediately started taking down the sail.

"Thanks," she called to Lucas while she worked.

Lucas glanced down at his dripping clothes, then over to the jacket that was halfway in the water, its fabric being ground against the sand by the lapping waves.

It occurred to Devin that she probably should have thought to pick it up for him. Whoops.

He paced over to retrieve it. "I cannot keep a suit clean around you people."

She couldn't tell if he was angry or joking.

Lexi had offered to lend Lucas a pair of sweatpants and a T-shirt left at her house by her oldest son. So, he stood in Devin's tiny shower rinsing off the lake water and sand, the plastic curtain brushing up against his skin every time he moved, while he struggled to keep his shins from hitting the steep sides of the narrow antique tub. The water temperature was erratic, the pressure pathetic, the taps whistled and a wire soap dish stuck out at a dangerous angle from the worn, tiled wall.

How did Devin put up with this every day of her life?

Rinsed clean, he cranked off the creaky taps and drew back the plastic curtain, scraping it noisily against the curved metal rod as he stepped from the deep tub onto a turquoise mat. The towels were small, with a pink floral pattern and a fringe at either end. He caught a glimpse of himself drying his hair in the steamy mirror, and he couldn't help but chuckle at the sight of roses topping his head.

He supposed a shave was out of the question. It was probably just as well. Given the lilac-scented soap he'd just used to wash, he needed the macho factor provided by a five-o'clock shadow. Fortunately, the sweatpants were black and the T-shirt was steel-gray.

It proved tricky getting dressed in the compact room. He knocked over a bottle of hand lotion with his elbow and banged his head on a low-lying lamp while he struggled into the slightly tight T-shirt. Then, having learned his lesson about waking up Amelia last time he was here, he carefully opened the aging bathroom door and padded silently out into the hall.

The house was quiet, but Devin's footfalls could be heard outside on the deck. As he rounded the corner into the living room, his nose picked up the scents of charcoal and grilling burgers through the screen of the patio door.

The sun had set while he showered. The lake was black now, except for the light from the few houses along the shoreline. A three-quarter moon hung low in the sky, while plastic patio lanterns glowed red, blue and green where they were strung on a wire around the perimeter of the deck.

Lucas started to smile at the classic backyard scene, but then he spotted Devin and instantly sobered. She stood at the barbecue, spatula in hand, watching the flames sear the burgers in front of her. Her feet were bare, legs long and tanned, and she wore a pair of lemon-yellow shorts paired with a white tank top that showed off her smooth golden shoulders.

She was in profile. Her hair was wispy short, waving softly

over her ears and along the nape of her neck. She was delicately beautiful in any setting, and his mind jumped swiftly back to those moments when he'd held her tight in his arms and kissed her luscious lips.

He didn't know why he'd let it happen. It was reckless and self-indulgent. But from that moment he'd brushed her shoulder in the dining room, kissing her had been all he could think about. Kissing her was still all he could think about.

She turned and spotted him standing there.

"All dry?" she called.

He moved to the screen door before answering, keeping his voice low, assuming Amelia must be asleep. "All dry," he confirmed.

She looked him up and down. "Who needs a six-thousand-dollar suit, anyway?"

He jokingly spread his arms. "Is it me?"

"It's you." She paused. "Surprisingly."

"Hey, I can hobnob with the common folk." Not that he could remember having done it recently. In fact, his last hamburger was probably at summer camp when he was in grade school. He was more a rib-eye kind of guy.

"Sure." She nodded sarcastically. "I bet you hobnob all the time."

He didn't answer, and instead slid open the screen door to join her.

"Would you like some wine?" she asked.

"Sounds great."

She pointed with the spatula. "On the counter next to the fridge. Bring me a glass, would you?"

"You got it," he answered easily, liking this laid-back side of Devin.

In the kitchen, after a few minutes of hunting for a bottle, Lucas realized she'd been referring to the cardboard box with the plastic spigot, sitting there on the kitchen counter. Wine in a box. Now that was a first.

He located a couple of stemmed glasses, then figured out how the spigot worked and filled them up.

He sniffed the bouquet, swirled it to check the legs and finally took an experimental sip of the deep burgundy liquid identified on the box as "Red Wine." It was a bit sharp, but not horribly objectionable. Probably not a lot of time for the tannins to mellow prior to the boxing process.

He gave a shrug as he lifted both glasses and headed back to the deck. When in Rome.

He set the wineglasses down on Devin's round table. It had a glass top and was surrounded by four thickly padded chairs.

"Can you grab the condiments?" she asked without turning from the grill.

"Sure."

"I'm toasting the buns," she called from behind him. "They were frozen. I hope you don't mind."

"I don't mind," he assured her. "Anything else you need from the kitchen?"

"Not that I can think of."

Lucas returned to the small kitchen and located mustard, ketchup and relish in the refrigerator.

He balanced them in his hands and ambled back to the deck once more, finding Devin setting toasted buns and burger patties on plastic plates on the round table.

"We'll need a knife," she told him.

He shot her a look of impatience. Had he not just asked if there was anything else?

"What?" she challenged.

"Why didn't you say something?"

"How did you expect to spread it on your bun? Oh, and grab the mayo, will you?"

He gave his head a shake.

"What's the matter, Lucas. You miss the serving staff?"

He kind of did. But he wasn't about to answer that. So instead, he retrieved a couple of knives and a jar of mayonnaise.

When he got back, Devin was folding her body into one of the padded chairs.

The wind had died down, leaving the air crystal clear above the water, accenting the view across the darkened lake.

"Thanks," she told him briskly, snagging one of the knives and starting to prepare her bun.

Lucas checked out the array of condiments and decided… what the heck? He loaded up his bun, adding a slice of cheese to boot.

The burger patty itself looked a little crisp on the outside, blackened in spots and shriveled rather small in comparison to the bun.

Devin took a big bite. "Mmm," she murmured in appreciation. "I'm starving."

"Busy day?" he asked. He'd followed Steve's LoJack beacon out here the minute he'd realized where the man was going. He had no intention of giving him time alone with Devin to indoctrinate her into the Steve Foster view of Pacific Robotics.

"Long time since lunch," she responded.

Lucas took a bite of his own burger. No meat in that section, but all in all, not bad.

"You sent Steve packing," she observed, biting down on a quarter-cut pickle.

Lucas swallowed, deciding to put his cards on the table. "Absolutely. He's trying to co-opt you to his side."

"And you?" she asked. "Are you trying to get me on your side?"

"Mine's the side of truth and justice," he responded.

Co-opting Devin was not his preferred plan. He needed a decisive win when it came to Amelia. He couldn't take the chance that Devin might support him now, and then later change her mind because someone had convinced her of the merits of a particular lame-assed project.

"Not from where I'm sitting," she told him.

"Yeah?" He was curious to hear how she'd couch his side versus Steve's.

"So far, of the two of you, Steve looks like the good guy."

Lucas set down his burger. "And you wonder why I have to fight you?"

The woman had absolutely no frame of reference. She was

a babe in the woods, vulnerable to whomever might sell her a bill of goods.

"We can compromise," she offered.

"You want me to compromise? You're so confused, you think *Steve* is the good guy." Lucas took a swallow of the wine. It really was pretty bad.

"If I made an agreement with you up front, I'd stick to it."

He didn't believe that. Not for one moment. "Until some point in the future when you disagreed with me."

Devin took another contemplative bite of her pickle. "I suppose that's true. I mean if you were really wrong about something."

She was everything he feared—erratic, unreliable and illogical.

Lucas pushed back his chair. "You are impossible."

"No. It's the situation that's impossible."

Lucas hated to admit it, but he could see her point. "I don't have an answer that's going to satisfy you," he admitted out loud. "All I know for sure is that *I* can trust me."

She gave a small, rueful smile. "And *I* can trust me."

They both stared at each other for a long moment of silence.

"Stalemate," he stated fatalistically.

"New topic," she told him, lifting her glass. "Nice rescue on the catamaran. Lexi asked me to thank you again."

"I haven't been sailing in a while," he answered, itching to continue the debate until she capitulated, but knowing the time wasn't right. "That part was fun."

"Sorry about the suit," Devin offered.

"Funny how I keep losing my clothes around you."

She glanced away, and he realized his double entendre had embarrassed her. Hell, he hadn't meant it that way. Not that he hadn't thought about it. Truth was, he had.

Damn it. Not good.

He took another sip of the wine. The taste seemed to be growing on him.

"Do you like sailing?" he asked, trying to bring the conversation onto some neutral ground.

She picked up the conversation thread, obviously relieved to move on. "Yes, I do. And Amelia seems to love it. She's a water baby."

"You'll have to come out on the Sound someday."

"You have a sailboat?"

"A little bigger than the catamaran," he said. "We'd probably have to bring a crew."

"A crew?"

"Three or four guys."

"Just how big is this sailboat?"

"Forty-six feet."

She chuckled. "Yeah, I'd say it's a little bigger than the catamaran."

"We could do dinner," he offered, knowing it sounded like a date, but not particularly caring. He found himself liking the idea of an evening sailing with Devin. And Steve certainly wouldn't be able to get his hands on her if they were on the water.

"With a boat that size, we could sail all the way to Vancouver."

"Sure," he said, shrugging. They could go wherever she liked.

She sat back in her chair, twirling her wineglass between her fingers. "It's some life you're living, Lucas Demarco."

Lucas glanced around the deck, realizing the homey atmosphere was growing on him. "It's a nice life you're living here, too."

"Not at the moment," she returned tartly.

He sighed. "You want to fight with me or accept my compliment on your house?"

"My house can't possibly impress you."

Lucas leaned forward, bracing his elbows on the table. "You, Devin Hartley, are an extraordinarily difficult person with whom to carry on a pleasant conversation."

She set down her glass and leaned forward to match his

posture. "And you, Lucas Demarco, are extraordinarily bad at hiding your condescension."

"I like your house," he protested. "Well, not the bathroom." He glanced up. "And these patio lanterns? Well, let's just say it's a good thing you're—"

He stopped himself.

Had he been about to tell her she was beautiful? What the hell was going on in his mind? "You have a great view." He gave a mock toast to the moon and the darkened lake.

She tipped her head back to look. "What's wrong with the lanterns?"

He checked out the faded plastic blobs, some of them warped, and the sagging wire where they hung. "They look like a fire hazard," he pointed out.

"My mother bought those lanterns."

Lucas didn't now how to respond to that.

Devin's voice rose. "My mother *loved* those lanterns."

"I'm uh…sorry?"

"Sorry that you insulted my home, or sorry that my mother has bad taste?"

There was something in her incredulous tone that didn't quite ring true, and Lucas realized she was fighting not to laugh.

"You're messing with me, aren't you?"

She grinned and shrugged her shoulders. "They came with the house," she admitted. "But *I* like them. They make it, I don't know, festive out here. It feels like we're having a party every night."

"Is that how you see life?" Lucas was genuinely curious. "One big party."

"This, from the playboy of the Pacific Northwest?"

"Playboy?" He raised his brows.

"I've seen the pictures. I've read the articles. Your party schedule is a lot fuller than mine." She waggled her finger at him. "You have had a very long list of girlfriends."

"Most of them were just dates."

"You mean one-night stands?"

"Like I'm going to tell you about my sex life."

She lowered her voice to a whisper, glancing dramatically from side to side. "Too embarrassing?"

He leaned closer. "Too boring."

A burst of laughter jumped out of her, and she rocked back in her chair. He noticed her wineglass was empty. So was his.

"That was *not* what I was expecting you to say," she admitted.

"More wine?" he asked, reaching for her glass.

She contemplated the question for a second. "Sure."

He rose to head back to the kitchen.

"Is this your way out of an embarrassing conversation?" she called after him.

He set the glasses down on her counter and refilled them, not about to shout back to her and wake Amelia.

But when he stepped back on the patio, she was clearly waiting to see how he'd respond.

"What's embarrassing about dating beautiful women?" He set both glasses down on the table.

"I was talking about your boring sex life."

"You going to tell me about yours?" he challenged.

"Nothing to tell."

"And that's not boring?" Truth was, he was more than intrigued by her answer. Nothing to tell? What did she mean by that?

"I'm taking care of a baby," she told him. "Not a lot of time left over for dating."

"And before that?" Amelia had only been Devin's responsibility for three months.

"Before that, my sister was going through a rough time. Your brother's fault, as you well know. The last thing she needed was to see me dressing up all bright and glittery, and prancing out the door to dance the night away with some random guy."

"All bright and glittery?" He kept it light, but he was intrigued by her decision to skip dating for months on end because of her sister. It had definitely not occurred to Lucas to give up dating because Konrad's marriage was in trouble.

"Jewelry," she explained. "Makeup, a dress, and I have this

cute little pair of high-heeled, rhinestone sandals." She lifted one of her bare feet, twisting it back and forth in the lantern light. "Perfect for dancing."

"You dress up?" So far, Lucas hadn't seen her in anything but casual cotton. Well, that and the bikini. Devin in that pale blue bikini was seared indelibly into his brain.

"I dress up damn good," she told him, wrinkling her nose and sipping her wine.

"Then we should get you a date."

She rolled her eyes. "Sure. Because that's exactly what's missing in my life right now."

"You wouldn't like to go out for dinner, a little dancing, maybe a play or a concert?"

"And leave Amelia?"

"We're getting a nanny, remember?"

Devin waved her glass for emphasis. "We are not hiring some Eastern European prison matron to run roughshod over poor little Amelia."

Lucas shook his head. He pushed the empty chair opposite Devin out to the side and propped his bare feet, lounging back. "You have a gift for hyperbole."

"I have veto power over the nanny."

"So do I."

"This ought to be interesting." She selected another quarter-slice of pickle and took a bite.

Lucas cringed at the taste combination of wine and pickles. Then again, the wine was nearly vinegar anyway. It was hard to believe he was on his second glass.

Devin propped one heel up on her chair, wrapping an arm around her upraised knee. "Dueling nannies," she joked.

"I've been invited to a charity ball Saturday night."

"Bully for you. Another gorgeous supermodel on your arm? You'd better give generously to make for your decadent behavior."

"It's for the children's hospital."

She crunched down on another bite of the pickle. "Then give more than generously."

"It's at the Saturna Club. A very hot ticket."

"Quit bragging."

"I'm not bragging."

"Yes, you are."

"I'm inviting you."

She drew back, swallowing, her expression registering stupefaction. *"What?"*

It was an excellent question. What the heck was he doing? Was he asking Devin on a date? Was he crazy? Was he so beguiled by the thought of seeing her dance in high-heeled, rhinestone sandals that he'd lost his mind?

"A girl needs to get out once in a while," he explained, carefully keeping his face impassive.

It was official. He'd lost his mind.

"I'm not going to date you."

"It's not a date. It's a charity ball. We'll be there to give away my money."

"Forget it." She rose from her chair, picking up her plate and her near empty glass.

He jumped up, putting a hand on her arm to stop her. Surely inviting her to a charity ball couldn't have made her that angry. "What's wrong?"

All the humor was gone from her sapphire eyes. "You're up to something," she accused.

"I'm not." He shook his head in denial, but that only made her eyes narrow in suspicion.

"There's not a single reason for you to invite me out."

"Then tell me what I'm up to." He knew he should take his hand off her arm now, but he really didn't want to. "What could I possibly gain by inviting you to a dance?"

She hesitated, and he could see her mind working over that one.

"Nothing." He answered his own question.

"Then why do it?"

Fair point. "Impulse," he answered honestly. "I was moved by your commitment to celibacy for the benefit of your sister. I found it sweet and self-sacrificing." Why didn't he shut up?

"You're not ending my celibacy, Lucas. No way, no how."

Lucas felt his jaw drop open. He'd had no intention... He hadn't even thought about... Okay, he'd thought about it, but that was only last night after their kiss, it had nothing to do with his invitation to the dance. Nothing.

"Your celibacy is safe with me," he told her, forcing himself to keep eyes front. If he gave in to temptation and let his gaze dip, she'd probably deck him. And she'd be justified.

She seemed to relax a bit. "Then you might want to stop salivating."

"Dream on."

She tilted her head. "You can't kiss me."

"I'm not going to kiss you." Did she mean right now, or at the dance?

"It's not a date," she warned.

"It's not a date," he agreed.

He could see her hesitating. "How many months since your last one?" he dared to ask.

Her blue eyes flared. "Don't rub it in."

"I'm trying to convince you to get out and have some fun." He forced himself to remove his hand from her arm and took a step back, giving her some space. "You're the one who thinks life should be a perpetual party."

"I didn't say that."

"Trust me, the Saturna Club will be way better than faded patio lanterns, wine in a box and burnt hamburger."

"The burgers weren't burnt."

He shot her a skeptical look.

She stuck her nose in the air. "They were well done, that's all."

He couldn't help but grin.

And she socked him in the arm. "Fine. I'll come to your stupid ball."

He chuckled. "Aren't you just the little charm school graduate?"

She stared to walk away. "I'm doing the dishes now."

He gathered up a load and followed her. "I'll do the dishes for you."

She called back over her shoulder, "Do you even know how?"

He did. Sort of. It had been a while. Probably quite a few years, now that he thought about it.

"You go sit down," he told her.

She looked tired. And he'd been reminded of how tough the last few months must have been for her. He didn't exactly feel guilty about her troubles, but he was willing to do the dishes for her.

To his surprise, she was finished fighting. She plopped herself down on the couch, pulled a pattered blanket over her bare legs and let him tackle the cleanup himself.

By the time he was finished, she'd fallen asleep right there on the worn striped sofa. It was nearly ten o'clock, and it was a long drive back for the three of them. They needed to get going.

He whispered her name, but she didn't stir.

He reached out to shake her, but he didn't have the heart.

Instead, he bundled her up with the blanket and carried her into her bedroom. Her feet were bare, and he caught himself gazing at her legs, the curve of her hip and her rounded breasts beneath the white tank top before he could bring himself to pull the quilt over her.

He could have easily left her there and headed home. He was certain she'd bring Amelia back to his place in the morning. But as he headed back down the hall, he found a small guest room, with a hard narrow bed, a white painted dresser and the ugliest gauzy curtains he'd ever seen. The blankets were scratchy, and the sheets were worn, but for some reason he couldn't think of anywhere else he wanted to be.

Five

Devin woke up in her own bed, disoriented because the sun was so high in the sky. Her first panicked thought was that something was wrong with Amelia.

But when she rushed to the baby's room and found the crib empty, she feared that Lucas might have taken her. Then she quickly discounted that idea, shaking her head to clear it of sleep. The man couldn't manage a multi-million dollar corporation if he was running for the border with a kidnapped baby.

Confused, and forcing herself to take a few breaths and stay calm, she headed for the living room.

It was empty.

But through the glass doors, down on the beach, she spotted Lucas, Lexi and Amelia. The two adults were perched on a log, while Amelia was digging her way through a pile of sand with a bright red shovel and bucket.

Lucas had stayed the night. And he'd let her sleep in.

For some reason, that knowledge nearly brought her to tears. It was silly. Everyone had some good qualities, and Lucas was no different. They drank wine last night. He probably didn't want to drive home. He'd obviously slept here and woken up with Amelia, keeping her quiet so that Devin could sleep in for the first time in three months.

She sniffed and swiped a frustrated hand under her eye.

Good grief. It wasn't as if the man had cured cancer.

She stumbled to the kitchen, found herself a mug and filled it with coffee, adding a heaping spoon of sugar. She was pretty sure Lexi must have brewed the coffee. Last night, Lucas had barely been able to figure out dish soap and hot water.

She pulled a light sweater over the T-shirt and shorts that she'd slept in and headed across the deck and down the long wooden staircase to the strip of lawn that ended at the sandy beach. Once there, she made her way toward Lexi and Lucas.

Amelia was the first to spot her, grinning and launching into a speedy crawl toward her. Lexi and Lucas both turned. They smiled in greeting, looking decidedly relaxed. Devin assumed Lexi's gratitude for the catamaran incident had tempered her opinion of Lucas.

"Good sleep?" asked Lexi with a grin.

"What time is it?" Devin hadn't thought to check. She knew she felt more rested than she had in months.

"Eleven," said Lucas.

"Seriously?"

He nodded.

"You got up with Amelia?" It was a little disconcerting that Devin hadn't heard them.

"Yes, I did." He yawned. "About 4:00 a.m. Then she slept on my chest for a while, but I didn't get much more sleep."

Devin could barely believe it. "Did you change her diaper?"

"There were instructions on the package."

"He got it on backward," Lexi elaborated.

Devin came down on her knees beside them in the sand. "And you fed her?"

Lucas rolled his eyes. "Quit sounding so amazed."

"It is amazing."

Amelia smacked her sandy hands against Devin's bare thighs.

"I gave her some juice and some Cheerios, and then Lexi came by."

"I really appreciate you letting me sleep in." Including both

Lucas and Lexi in the thank-you, Devin held her coffee mug over to the side and out of harm's way. "I feel pretty great."

"Lexi's agreed to babysit for us," said Lucas.

"I hear you two are going on a date," said Lexi.

"It's not a date," Devin quickly corrected. Had she really agreed to go to the dance with him tomorrow night? What had she been thinking? "Lucas is trying to co-opt me with, I don't know, fine food and a waltz around the dance floor, so that I won't support Steve."

Lucas turned to Lexi. "See what I mean?"

Lexi nodded her understanding.

"What?" Devin glanced back and forth between the two.

"He thinks you're suspicious," said Lexi.

"Of course I'm suspicious," Devin retorted. "So are you. And we're justified in our suspicions." She looked back and forth again. "What exactly did I miss here?"

Lucas stood up from his perch on the log, brushing the sand from the back of the borrowed sweatpants. "I've got a meeting," he told them. "And I think I'd better get home and change first." His glance went to Devin. "See you there later?"

"Sure," she answered. She should thank him again for letting her sleep. But for some reason she hesitated to show him too much gratitude. She didn't want him to think she liked him. She didn't. Well, she kind of did this morning. But it wasn't anything permanent.

Everything suddenly seemed confusing.

He bent over and gave Amelia a little rub on the head, then gave them all a careless wave as he started back across the beach to the lawn and the staircase.

"Tell me *everything*," breathed Lexi.

"There's nothing to tell," Devin responded, moving to the spot on the log that Lucas had vacated. She'd have to clean up and get back to the Demarcos soon, but she had a few more minutes to enjoy the tranquility of her own home. "I had a great sleep."

"Alone?"

Devin twisted her head to stare at Lexi. "Of course I was alone. What did he tell you?"

"Nothing." Lexi shook her head. "But I couldn't exactly ask him, could I?"

"Is *that* why you were being nice to him?"

Lexi had had a pretty remarkable change in attitude over a boat rescue.

"He's not as bad as I expected," said Lexi.

Devin understood what her friend meant. There was something disarmingly charming about Lucas. Then again, that's exactly what Monica had thought about Konrad—that he was misunderstood, nicer than people realized, not quite the cold, hard-ass the media made him out to be. It was a dangerous road to go down.

"He's trying to take Amelia away from me," Devin reminded Lexi.

"Challenge him to a diapering contest in the courtroom. You'll win."

"This isn't a joke."

Lexi sobered and gazed out across the sparkling water. "I know. It's heart-wrenching. I find myself wishing he was more of a jerk, then I could hate him."

"You don't have to hate him." Devin gazed out across the water herself. A few powerboats streamed along in front of the far shore, white wakes streaking out behind them. Now that the sun was warm, most of the beaches were coming alive with residents. "I just have to beat him."

Lexi covered her hand. "You will."

"I'm not so sure."

Silently, they stared at the lake.

"So," said Lexi, "what's up with the dancing?"

"I can't remember how it started." Devin sat up straighter on the log. "But I mentioned how long it had been since I'd had a date."

"And he stepped up to the plate?"

"He's up to something." Devin knew she should be annoyed by the way he'd managed to manipulate her into doing something she just knew she would regret. But she couldn't help but smile at the thought of a fancy party. "It'll be nice to dress up again," she admitted. "And I made him promise not to kiss me."

"Seriously?"

"Yes."

"You said that out loud?"

Devin gave a decisive nod. She didn't want there to be any misunderstanding. The very last thing she needed was another go-round in Lucas's arms. She banished the unwanted image and tamped down her wayward hormonal reaction. It would be a catastrophic mistake to kiss Lucas.

Okay, so technically, she was in Lucas's arms again. But they were dancing, and it was all very proper. There was a good nine inches of space between them. Lucas's dance frame was appropriate, and his lead was smooth and confident. He was also devastatingly handsome in his tux. No surprise there.

The ballroom at the Saturna Club was opulent and spacious. It had thirty-foot ceilings, with a marble pillar perimeter around the rectangular dance floor. The chandeliers were lavish, the flowers fresh, and dinner had featured fresh Pacific salmon and white chocolate mousse served with an impressive flare by what must have been a hundred efficient, tuxedoed waiters.

One long side of the ballroom opened to a concrete patio that overlooked Puget Sound. The crisp ocean breeze wafted in. Cruise ships, freighters and smaller boats passed by, while the lights of Bainbridge Island twinkled off in the distance.

After months of drool and diapers, Devin felt like a fairy princess. She'd even splurged on a new dress—though she'd never admit to Lucas that she'd gone shopping. It was strapless, copper satin, with a fitted top that shimmered against her skin, and a full skirt that rustled at her knees. She'd worn the rhinestone sandals and borrowed a silver link necklace and matching earrings from Lexi. The earrings dangled from her lobes, gently brushing against her neck as she danced.

It was fun to feel pretty.

"The nanny interviews start at ten in the morning," Lucas reminded her as they moved into a turn.

Devin frowned up at him. "You're ruining the mood."

"There's a mood?"

"Of *course* there's a mood. We have music, fine food, champagne—"

"And beautiful women." His eyes lit up with a appreciative smile that bordered on mischief.

"Handsome men," she returned, refusing to react.

"Thank you."

"Plural," she corrected. "I was talking in general."

"Well, I wasn't."

Her steps faltered. This wasn't where she'd wanted the conversation to go.

"You look very beautiful, Devin."

Though she knew she should, she couldn't bring herself to look away from him, and it was a struggle to maintain her equilibrium. He was being polite, nothing more. It was appropriate to compliment a woman while escorting her for the evening. He didn't mean she was beautiful in, say, comparison to the supermodels and trophy wives in ten-thousand-dollar dresses who were swirling around the room.

He leaned down to whisper in her ear. "I believe the words you're looking for are *thank you*."

Her throat was dry, but she swallowed to clear it. "Thank you."

He smiled and straightened.

"That wasn't fair," she admonished.

Amusement still lurked in his eyes. "Not fair?"

This time, she was the one who leaned in. "You promised."

"Not to compliment you?"

"Not to…" She struggled for the right words. "This isn't supposed to be a date."

"You didn't want to talk about nannies," he responded with a shrug, like there were only two topics in the world.

"Fine. Let's talk about nannies."

"And spoil the mood?"

"Please. Go ahead and spoil the mood." She didn't care that she sounded petulant.

The danger in pretending she was a princess was that it made Lucas the prince. And it was all too easy to let the fantasy meander into perilous territory.

They'd arrived at the party tonight in a limo. Later, they'd go home to his castle. And if she wasn't careful, she'd start thinking about a kiss good-night.

"The interviews begin at ten," he said.

She shook off her wayward thoughts. "Not with the prison matrons."

"I gave the agency both your specifications and mine. They're sending people who are available immediately."

She supposed she'd have to be content with that.

They danced a few more steps, swaying under shimmering lights.

"Did you have a nanny?" she found herself asking.

"Yes, I did," he told her. "Several of them."

"And did you like them?"

"Sometimes."

"What does that mean?"

"It means I was little boy. Nannies don't like little boys to climb trees, throw rocks, jump bicycles and climb on the garage roof."

Devin couldn't help but smile at the images. "I take it you did all those things anyway?"

"Those and more. And so did Konrad. Looking back, I'm thinking that might be why we went through so many nannies." The small orchestra switched to a slower song, and Lucas settled her a bit closer. "What about you?"

Devin shook her head. "No nanny for the Hartleys."

"What were you like as a kid?"

"I don't know. Normal, I guess."

"Did you grow up at Lake Westmire?"

"Same house I live in now. With my mom and Monica. We

swam, built sand castles, baked cookies, designed elaborate dollhouses all over the yard."

Devin had moved away from Lake Westmire to attend college. She came back five years ago when her mother was diagnosed with cancer. But tonight wasn't the time to think about that.

Instead, she fixed her memories on their teenage years. Monica had been a year younger, and the neighborhood had been full of kids around their ages.

"When we were teenagers," she continued, remembering, "Monica and I sat with our friends around weekend bonfires down at the park by Sunny Bay."

"And kissed the boys?" Lucas asked in a teasing tone.

"Tommy McGuire," Devin admitted. "Ninth grade. It was a dare, and he cut my nose with his glasses."

Lucas laughed at that.

"I bet your first kiss wasn't perfect, either," she retorted.

"You be the judge. I have videotape."

"Are you kidding me?"

"Steve secretly took it. He threatened to show my mother, until I beat the crap out of him and took the camera away."

"You beat up Steve?"

"He was a Peeping Tom. I'm surprised he didn't grow up to be a member of the paparazzi."

"He was a kid."

"He hasn't changed."

"Is this another of your warnings about the evil Steve?"

"No. This is an offer for you to review the game tape and tell me what you think of my first kiss."

Devin chuckled low, even while she shook her head. "I'm not watching a videotape of your first kiss."

"Why not? Maybe you could give me some pointers."

"I'm sure your technique has changed considerably since you were… How old were you?"

"I don't remember." His gaze shifted to her lips, and she could tell from the glow in his gray eyes exactly what he was remembering.

She was remembering it, too.

"Lucas." A hearty male voice interrupted the moment.

Lucas glanced to the side, while Devin tamped down the buzz of sexual awareness lighting up her body.

"Mr. Mayor." After what felt like a brief hesitation, Lucas let go of Devin to shake the man's hand.

"I wanted to thank you personally for your generous donation to the hospital." The mayor's curious glance went to Devin for a brief second.

The man was in his midfifties. His full head of distinguished gray hair topped a tall physique that he kept in shape through highly publicized biking and rowing sessions.

"Mr. Mayor, this is Devin Hartley."

"Ms. Hartley." The mayor took her hand and gave it a gentle shake.

Nobody acknowledged or introduced the well-groomed man standing behind and to the left of the mayor. Devin assumed he was either an aide or security.

"It's a pleasure to meet you," said Devin. "This is a wonderful party."

"We have the hospital board to thank for that," the mayor responded as he released her hand. "And we have donors like Lucas to thank for the new pediatric wing. Please, enjoy yourselves tonight. You'll be at the ground-breaking next weekend?" he asked Lucas.

"Wouldn't miss it," Lucas responded.

With a final nod, the mayor withdrew.

The band had started a break, and a recorded, soft rock song wafted through the speakers.

"Thirsty?" asked Lucas, stepping close, one hand going to the small of her back as the crowd made their way off the dance floor.

"Sure," she responded, taking his lead back toward their table. "I take it you gave a big donation?" She couldn't help wondering if her words at the barbecue had influenced Lucas on that front.

"Pacific Robotics made a big donation," Lucas corrected. "That includes Amelia."

Was it thousands? Tens of thousands? *Hundreds* of thousands? "How did you decide? I mean, how do you decide how much to donate?"

"It's tough," Lucas acknowledged. He flagged a passing waiter and they ordered a bottle of sparkling water. "I bet we get a dozen requests a week from worthy charitable organizations. And from scam artists, of course."

"That many?" Devin hadn't given any thought to that side of being in business.

They arrived back at their table. All eight of the chairs were vacant, and Lucas pulled out the one draped with Devin's light wrap.

She sat down. "I assume you say no to most of them?"

"If you didn't, you'd be bankrupt in a year. For better or worse, you have to pick your priorities, allocate an appropriate sum of money and hope what you're doing helps out."

Devin found herself admiring this side of Lucas.

"Amelia needs to learn this," he continued, gaze going thoughtful. "This and about a million other things. I don't want to sound patronizing, but there are complexities to running a corporation that you couldn't possibly imagine."

Devin tried not to bristle. "How could that possibly sound patronizing?"

He gave a hard sigh.

"Is this the latest sales pitch for you as her guardian?" Devin asked.

"This is context to help you understand why I'm doing what I'm doing. This isn't a game, Devin. Hundreds of millions… billions of dollars are at stake. Jobs for people in five different countries. The well-being of the family."

"I don't think the Demarcos are doing too badly."

"And it's going to be partly up to Amelia to see that many more generations of Demarcos keep the corporation healthy. It's not just about boats and sports cars. It's about hospitals and scholarships and ordinary peoples' livelihoods."

"She's nine months old, Lucas."

He paused, and some of the intensity went out of his eyes.

The waiter arrived, opening the ornate bottle of water and pouring it into two glasses over ice.

"You're right," said Lucas as the man left the table. "Before she decides if animal welfare is more important than inner-city youth programs, we need to get her potty trained and teach her to use a knife and fork. Back to the nanny conversation."

"Before the weight of the world crashes down on the poor girl's shoulders, we need to let her have a little fun." Devin raised her glass for a sip. "Back to the nanny conversation."

Devin clipped the portable baby monitor into the waistband of her jeans as she pulled the door shut between Amelia's nursery and the ensuite that connected it to her own bedroom in the mansion. She'd promised Lucas they could discuss what they'd each thought of this morning's nanny interviews once Amelia was down for her afternoon nap.

On the way past the mirror, Devin checked her reflection. Her hair was messy from Amelia playing with it, and she had a streak of dirt across one cheek. Who knew where that had come from. And the left shoulder of her blue T-shirt was one big wet blob where Amelia had sucked on it while rocking to sleep.

Telling herself it wasn't vanity, and it certainly wasn't because she cared about Lucas's opinion, it was simply good grooming, she pulled a hairbrush from the vanity drawer and dragged it through her hair. Then she gave her face a quick wash, rubbing in some moisturizer with sunscreen, in case they decided to chat on the porch.

Finally, on her way back into her own room, she grasped the bottom hem of her T-shirt to pull it—

She stumbled to a halt. "Steve?"

The man was standing in front of her bedroom window, curtain lifted with his left hand, gazing out at the ocean.

"Hi, Devin." He turned his head.

"You startled me."

He'd also annoyed her. What did he think he was doing lingering around her bedroom?

And he'd closed the door behind him.

Okay, that was just creepy.

"I need to talk to you." He let the curtain drop, and his cold expression did nothing to make her feel better.

"Can we do it in the hall?" she asked, moving toward the bedroom door. "Amelia just fell asleep."

Devin wasn't exactly frightened, but it was definitely disconcerting to have him invade her space this way.

"I'd rather talk in private," he said.

Well, she'd rather talk in public. She didn't stop moving.

"What happened after I left?" There was a trace of impatience in his tone.

Devin paused with her hand on the doorknob, turning back. "After you left what?"

"Your house. The other day. I know he stayed."

"Lucas?"

"Yes, Lucas."

"He was soaking wet."

Steve had stayed long enough to hear Lexi offer Lucas the use of her son's clothes.

"He was there all night," Steve accused, anger flaring in his dark eyes.

Okay, he'd gone way over the line with that crack. Devin was getting angry. She twisted the knob. "I think you'd better leave."

Steve took a couple of steps toward her, putting his hand up to block the door shut. "This isn't your home, Devin."

She didn't bother answering.

"You're a smart woman. You have to know what he's doing. You have to know you're going to get hurt."

"That's none of your business." She didn't know what Steve suspected about her relationship with Lucas. But she wasn't about to explain herself.

He paused beside her, lowering his voice, eyes cool and detached. "I tried to make this easy for you. I offered my help. I paid for your lawyers."

"Lucas slept on the couch, Steve." She didn't know why she bothered telling him that. It wasn't because she was trying to change his mind about helping her. As of this second, she wasn't taking anything from Steve ever again.

He shook his head. "It would have worked, Devin."

She was tempted to ask what would have worked, but she held her tongue. The sooner this conversation was over, the better.

"This might not be my house—" she steeled her strength and looked him directly in the eyes "—but it is my room for the time being, and I'm asking you to leave."

He stared down at her. There was a chill in his brown eyes that sent a shiver straight up her spine.

But after a long pause, he stepped back, and so did she. He reached for the door, opened it and left without a word. She swiftly closed it behind him and found her hand shaking and her stomach in knots.

She stood in the bedroom for a few minutes, wondering what to do next.

Then she heard a car start up in the driveway below. She moved to the window to watch Steve pull away. Once his taillights disappeared beneath the canopy of oaks tress, she breathed a sigh of relief, pulling her shirt over her head.

She changed into a white sleeveless blouse, tucked her feet into a pair of worn sandals, then headed downstairs to find Lucas.

He was on the deck off the great room, sitting on a padded chair at one of the round tables that overlooked the yard. Fruit and croissants had been served, along with a carafe of coffee. Lucas was sipping a cup.

"She asleep?" he asked, rising briefly as Devin took the chair opposite.

Devin nodded, debating whether to tell him about the bizarre conversation with Steve. Though she was becoming more inclined to trust Lucas over Steve, she wasn't really ready to trust anyone in this strange family. Besides, how would it help to tell Lucas? He already thought Steve was plotting against him, which he was. Nothing new there.

"I thought nanny number three had potential," said Lucas, holding up the coffee carafe in a question.

Devin pushed her cup toward him to say yes. "Was she the one with the braid?"

"No. The one in the hat."

"No uniforms," said Devin, adding sugar to her coffee.

Lucas lifted the plate of croissants, offering them to Devin. "What's wrong with uniforms?"

She took a croissant. "I don't like them."

"So, you're going to have a dress code?"

"No. A uniform would be a dress code. I don't want Amelia to feel like she's in an institution."

"A uniform is only a dress code if it's not optional. By banning uniforms you are, in fact, instituting a dress code."

"You're being deliberately obtuse. The nanny can wear anything she wants."

"Unless it's a uniform."

Devin tore into her croissant. "Nobody wants to wear a uniform."

Lucas selected a grape. "You can't possibly know that."

"I liked the one with the braid," said Devin. She took a sip of the hot coffee. "I think her name was Beverly."

Lucas's phone rang. He checked the number and then pushed a button, turning his attention back to Devin. "She seemed disorganized to me."

"How so?"

"First off, she was late. And then that big, ugly orange purse with—"

"You're giving demerits for style?"

"You did."

Static crackled on the baby monitor.

A man's muffled voice came over the speaker. The words were indistinct, but Devin felt her entire body go cold.

The man spoke again.

Steve.

She swore out loud, jumped up and shoved her chair out of the way. It clattered to the floor of the deck.

She took off running through the great room, down the hall

to the foyer and the main staircase, while Lucas called out her name, rushing behind her.

She pounded up the stairs and sprinted down the hall. Then she rounded the corner to find two male staff members chatting outside Amelia's nursery. The doors to both rooms were closed, and the men looked up in surprise at Devin's entrance.

She quickly brushed passed them and cracked open the nursery door.

Amelia was sound asleep and completely alone.

"Is everything all right, ma'am?" one of the men asked.

"Devin?" Lucas's voice came from the end of the hall.

Devin's heart was pounding and her lungs drew in deep breaths. She gathered her wits. "Everything's fine."

Lucas marched forward.

"Can you please excuse us?" he asked the two men.

They quickly withdrew.

"What the hell?" Lucas demanded, voice low. "You're white as a ghost."

"It's okay," Devin gasped. The men's voices outside the nursery had obviously been picked up by the monitor.

"What happened?"

"I thought—" she began, wondering how much to tell him. She realized she was going to sound like a hysterical idiot. But she couldn't come up with anything to replace the truth.

"You thought *what?*"

"Steve was here," she admitted.

Lucas's brows knit together in obvious confusion. "You thought Steve was here?"

"No," Devin corrected. "Steve *was* here. Earlier. I came out of the nursery and found him in my room."

Lucas's brows drew together. His eyes went stormy, and his mouth thinned.

"He seemed annoyed that you'd stayed over at my place. He knew you were there all night, and—"

"Hold on a minute," Lucas interrupted. "Did he tell you that, or did you tell him?"

"He told me." Devin resented the implication that she'd

rushed to Steve with the news. Then again, why should Lucas trust her any more than she trusted him?

She continued, suddenly wanting to get the whole story out. "Then he said he had tried to make this easy for me. I got the impression he wasn't going to make it easy for me anymore. I didn't know what he meant. But then I heard a man's voice." She paused. "On the baby monitor. And for a minute, I thought…"

"You thought Steve might harm Amelia?"

"I thought he'd come back. Beyond that, I didn't know what to think."

Lucas wrapped a large, warm hand over her shoulder and gave a gentle squeeze. "Steve is not going to hurt Amelia."

Devin nodded, but it was only to be agreeable. Her radar was up when it came to Steve. If she had her way, he'd never be near Amelia again.

"I mean, even if he would, which believe me, he wouldn't. He's a jerk, but he'd never go that far. We'll increase security, Devin. We can get Amelia a bodyguard instead of a nanny if it makes you feel better."

Devin closed her eyes and took a deep, cleansing breath.

"Okay?" he asked.

She gave a jerky nod.

His hand tightened on her shoulder, and the next thing she knew, she was being drawn into his embrace.

"It's going to be fine," he promised her in a gruff voice.

His arms felt wonderfully strong as they wrapped around her. His chest felt broad and solid against her cheek. And though she knew depending on Lucas was the most dangerous thing she could do, for just a moment, she let herself sink into his strength.

Lucas couldn't bring himself to believe that Steve was a real danger to Amelia. But he was beyond furious with him for approaching and intimidating Devin. And he'd done it right here in the mansion. The man's audacity knew no bounds.

Lucas had immediately contacted Theodore Vick, the Demarcos' head of security and assigned extra full-time protection to Devin and Amelia. He'd also talked to Byron about Steve pulling his legal support from Devin and what it could mean. Despite his down-home manner, Byron was a shrewd strategist, with an impressive network of contacts and a gift for sleuthing out information. If anyone could ferret out Steve's new plan, it was Byron.

Now, Byron appeared in the doorway of Lucas's office on the lower floor of the mansion.

"Anything?" asked Lucas without preamble. He'd spent the morning trying to focus on a problem with new high-tech foreign ownership regulations in Sweden. But he hadn't had much success forgetting about either Devin or Steve.

Byron shut the door behind him and entered the room. "Did Steve's mama drop him on his head when he was a baby?" he asked conversationally.

Lucas wasn't sure how to interpret that question, so he didn't offer an answer.

"If not, she should have," said Byron. "There is something terribly wrong with that boy."

Lucas stood from his chair and came around the desk that was positioned at one end of the rectangular room. The sliding glass doors were open to a small patio, and Byron motioned for him to pull them shut.

Now Lucas was very curious. "What did you find out?"

"You remember this?" Byron tossed a red-labeled videotape on the square meeting table that took up one corner of the room.

"Is that the one from Granddad's will?"

Byron gave a curt nod. "Let's just refresh your memory a tad, shall we?" He slid the tape into the old VCR that was connected to Lucas's television set. Then he took up the remote and gestured to the chairs around the meeting table.

"Did we miss something the first time through?" asked Lucas, lowering himself into one of the charcoal-gray, sling-back leather chairs.

"It was right there under our noses the whole time." Byron

pressed a button on the remote, and a poorly lit picture came up on the screen.

It was a younger-looking Granddad, sitting in this same office, vintage railway photos on the wall in the background.

Byron fast-forwarded through part of the tape.

"Here we go," he said, switching the video back to Play.

Granddad's familiar, gravelly voice came through the twin speakers. "The reason for this is that you boys need to understand the difference between work and family. This great company you've inherited was built on a foundation of family. Your grandmothers and great-grandmothers may not have had their names on the stationery, but they played pivotal roles in the building of what is now Pacific Robotics." His old eyes softened. "Lucy was my rock. She was there through good times and bad, through success and failure, always believing I could do the impossible. And, you boys, you need to find your own rocks." Granddad folded his hands on the desk and leaned toward the camera. "And if leaving my estate to a future great-grandchild gives you inspiration to get out there and look, so be it. I can live with that."

Byron clicked a button to stop the tape.

"I don't get it," said Lucas, tapping the tabletop in front of him. "We've seen this all before. What's the point?"

"You gotta want it," said Byron. "Look between the lines. That's what Steve did."

Lucas gave his head a small shake, still not following.

"Steve and his lawyers have rustled up a set of legal precedents for videotapes being used as a preamble to a will."

Lucas gestured to the blank screen. "Granddad only reiterated that his firstborn great-grandchild inherits."

Byron nodded. "You got that right. Your granddaddy hoped you boys would find yourselves some pretty gals, fall in love, get married and have children."

"Yes, he did," Lucas sighed in exasperation. It was a ridiculous way to structure an inheritance.

His grandfather should have left his shares to the person who would do the best job of managing the company. This crap about family being the rock of a man's existence was just the ramblings of an old man. Single men could be great managers, and married men could be terrible managers. There was much more to it than marital status.

"And Steve has entered a brand-new petition that asks for this videotape to be considered the spirit of your granddaddy's will."

"He can do that?" As far as Lucas was concerned, the will was already settled.

"It appears as though he can," said Byron. "It seems the court can decide to balance the letter of a will with the spirit of a will."

"But, the shares are already in Amelia's name."

"It's like an appeal."

"He could get the will overturned?"

"He might. He's swearing Konrad only married Monica to get the gal pregnant. That's a clear violation of the spirit of the will. And Steve's got a lot of lawyers hunting up precedents to back him."

"Amelia could lose her shares?"

She could.

"Seriously?"

"Yes."

"Does he have a chance in hell?"

"I'm told he does. And it gets worse."

Lucas paused, eyes narrowing.

"His star witness?" asked Byron. "The person who'll get up there and testify that Konrad and Monica's marriage was a sham?"

Lucas brought the end of his fist down on the table, rattling the water glasses as he swore out loud.

Byron nodded.

"Devin," said Lucas.

"Devin," Byron confirmed. He rose and ejected the tape from the machine, stuffing it back into its cardboard cover. "When she takes you on over custody, that lady will sit up there on that witness stand and hand Steve his evidence on a silver platter."

Six

Devin had said yes when Lucas offered to join her on her evening jog around the grounds. She was still rattled from her encounter with Steve, and company didn't seem like such a bad idea.

A security guard was posted in the hallway outside the nursery, and one of the housekeepers was watching the new video baby monitor. Deep down, Devin knew it was overkill. But she didn't care. It was hard to forget the fact that Steve had simply sauntered into the mansion and into her room.

She realized he was a member of the Demarco family, so there was no reason for anyone to stop him. But Lucas assured her the staff had been instructed to announce all guests, including family members, from here on in.

They'd followed the pot-lighted mulch pathway as it wound through the grounds. In contrast to the last time they'd jogged, Lucas kept his pace easy, chatting about maintenance on his sailboat and upcoming events for the new hospital wing. Devin found herself relaxing.

They rounded the stables, where two tall chestnut horses stood near the rail.

"Do you ride?" she asked, her breathing heavy.

"Occasionally. Byron's the family cowboy. He's got quite the spread down there in Texas, and he's firmly committed to the country lifestyle. I half expect him to show up with a few steers one of these days. Apparently, we have some grazing potential on the north side of the property."

Devin took in Lucas's jogging short and runners. "Somehow, I can't see you riding the range."

"What? You don't think I'd look good in a Stetson?"

Actually, she assumed he'd look great in a Stetson. But that wasn't something she was prepared to think about, much less talk about. "I don't think you'd like the dust."

"True enough," he said, and nodded. "Give me a clean shirt, a hot babe and the Bugatti, and I'm in my element."

"Or a set of polished clubs and a golf cart?"

"That'd work, too," he agreed. "What about you? You golf?"

Devin shook her head. "I do not."

"You want to try?"

"Not particularly." Of all the places she could put her leisure time and recreational resources, she couldn't say golf had ever made it to the top of her list.

"It's a lot of fun," he cajoled.

"My life's a little too busy to take up an expensive, time-consuming sport."

"I thought you were the party girl."

"That was *your* opinion. I've got a book deadline to meet and a baby to care for. Barbecue dinners I can do. Golf games, not so much."

"What about swimming?" he asked, nodding as they approached the pool and the end of their run.

"Sure, I swim. I live on a lakeshore."

"I meant right now. I'm sweltering."

They slowed to a walk as they moved onto the pool deck. Lucas swiped the back of his hand across his sweaty forehead.

Devin was hot, too. And the pool looked inviting. But she had no desire to head up to the second floor and retrieve her bathing suit. When she crossed the threshold of her bedroom tonight, she'd have only one thing in mind, and that was sleep.

"No suit," she told him, placing her hand on one of the tables for balance and stretching out a calf muscle.

"No problem." He pulled his phone from the pocket of his shorts.

"You are *not* calling the staff to bring me a bathing suit."

"Who said anything about a bathing suit?" He set the phone down on a table and stripped off his shirt, tossing it onto a lounger.

Devin couldn't help but take in a quick glimpse of his bare chest. The man was in amazing shape.

But then he reached for the waistband of his shorts.

She pulled her leg from the stretch position and staggered back. "Whoa. Hang on there, cowboy."

He grinned unrepentantly. "Boxers," he assured her. "But I can dim the lights if you're shy."

She withdrew a few more paces. "It's all yours. I'll just head up to my room."

"Don't be ridiculous." He crossed to the pool house and opened an electrical panel, flipping a couple of switches, and the pool water went dark, as did the deck area. Illumination came from discrete pot lights placed in the shrubbery and flower gardens around the perimeter of the pool.

"Come on—" he gave her a cajoling wave and moved forward in the darkness "—you must be sweltering."

"I'm not wearing boxers," she answered tartly, half-scandalized and half-aroused at the thought of a late night swim with Lucas.

"You naked under those shorts?" He reached for his waistband again, and she swiftly looked away.

"I am not."

"Then swim in your underwear. It's no different than a bikini."

"Yes, it is."

"Only in your mind."

She heard a splash, and caught him in her peripheral vision as he sliced into the deep end. His boxers flashed black before he disappeared into the dark water.

He came up, shaking his wet hair. "It's beautiful," he enthused. "I'll even be a gentleman and turn around until you get in the water."

She had to admit, the water looked incredibly tempting. It was unseasonably warm, and Devin had been hot all day, running errands around town. Amelia had been fussy, and Devin's car's air conditioner was dying a slow but final death.

She reached for a bottle of chilled water and took a drink, cooling her parched throat. The liquid helped, but it really didn't do the trick. She was very tempted by the pool.

"You promise you won't look?" she called to him.

He turned his back on her. "Don't be paranoid."

Devin drew a breath, glancing around at the dimly lit yard. There was no one else out here, and the house was far enough away that they wouldn't be seen, at least not in any detail, especially with the lights out. Her peach-colored bra and panties would be indistinguishable from a bikini. It wasn't as if they were going skinny-dipping, she told herself. And it would feel fantastic to cool off before she headed up to bed.

"Okay," she announced, kicking off her shoes. "I'm coming in." She quickly peeled off her sweaty T-shirt and her running shorts. She mostly trusted Lucas to keep his word, but she wasn't taking any chances. She dove straight into the pool.

After an initial shock of cold, the water felt heavenly. She broke the surface and smoothed her hair back from her face, treading water at the opposite side of the deep end from Lucas.

"Nice?" he asked, his voice a low rumble and his face a dark silhouette against the pot lights in the distant gardens.

"Very nice," she agreed, doing an easy front stroke down the length of the pool. She tried to pretend it was just another swim, but she was hyperaware of the darkness, her silky underwear and Lucas's gaze following her as she swam.

The memory of their kiss battered its way into her brain. And she couldn't seem to banish the feel of his arms around her. Maybe it was a forbidden-fruit syndrome. Or maybe she was learning all the reasons Monica had been unable to resist Konrad, despite all the evidence he was bad news.

Lucas was definitely bad news for Devin. She understood that with every fiber of her being. But it didn't seem to stop her from wanting him. It didn't even stop her from making stupid decisions like this little late-night swim.

Oh, those Demarco men were good.

"Devin?" It was Lucas's deep voice, strumming along her nervous system.

"Yes?" she answered, finding her feet in the chest-deep water and resting her hand on the smooth pool wall as she turned to look at him.

He'd drifted closer then stood, water dripping down his skin. "There's something you and I need to talk about."

"What?" she asked warily, hoping it didn't have anything to do with the fact that she was in her underwear and they were taking a late-night swim, or the kiss they'd shared two days ago.

But he looked serious, and not the least bit flirtatious.

Despite everything, she was forced to squelch a flash of disappointment. She warned herself to get a grip. She did not want him to flirt with her. She dreaded the idea that he might try to flirt with her.

"It's about Steve," he said, voice going lower as he moved closer still.

Devin's stomach reflexively clenched with anxiety. She didn't want to talk about Steve. She didn't even want to think about Steve.

"Byron and I figured out his new tactic."

Devin swallowed. "Is it bad?" Did she need to worry?

"It's quite despicable," said Lucas, rubbing his palm across his face to remove the errant water droplets. The beads on his skin made him look rakish and dangerous. "He's trying to have Amelia disinherited."

Devin focused her attention. "How do you mean?"

"Steve is trying to prove she isn't entitled to the ten percent of Pacific Robotics."

"How can he do that?"

"He's found a loophole in the will," said Lucas. "He thinks if he can prove Konrad and Monica's marriage was a sham—"

"It was a sham," Devin felt compelled to point out.

Lucas crossed his arms over his muscular chest. "It wasn't. But that's not the point."

Devin didn't answer, assuming Lucas would only let her wait so long before he told her exactly what the point was.

"The point is—" he drew a deep breath "—you might inadvertently help him."

"Inadvertently?" What planet had Lucas been living on these past few weeks. "If the point he's making is that Monica and Konrad's marriage was a sham, then I'll be helping him on purpose."

Lucas took a step forward, his head cocking slightly to one side. "You can't do that, Devin."

"I'm not going to lie, Lucas."

"I'm not asking you to lie."

"Konrad didn't love Monica."

"He *did* love her."

Devin clenched down on her jaw. If Amelia was entitled to the inheritance, Devin would fight tooth and nail for her. But if she wasn't…

"You don't have some special psychic ability to see into Konrad's brain," said Lucas.

"Don't you mean into his heart?"

"You need to see the broader picture."

"That's a nice way to put it."

"You need to allow for the possibility, *however slim,* that you might have been mistaken about Konrad."

"I don't *need* to do anything." The truth was the truth.

"Listen to me—"

"You're grasping at straws." Devin had spent countless nights consoling Monica over Konrad's betrayal. He'd hurt her sister very badly, and Devin wasn't about to pretty it up now.

"Amelia is the legal and rightful heir of my grandfather's will," Lucas growled. "You and I…" He paused, clearly gathering his emotions. "*You and I* owe it to Konrad and to Monica and to my grandfather to protect Amelia's interests." Lucas's shoulders were squared, his jaw was set in a determined line and his eyes glittered black in the dim light.

When Devin didn't respond, Lucas carried on. "And that means you and I have to stop fighting with each other."

"We're not fighting." Well, maybe they were at this very moment. But they'd been getting along pretty well over the past couple of days. In fact, they'd been getting along too well for Devin's peace of mind.

"I mean over the guardianship case," said Lucas. "We have to shut it down."

It took a second for his words to sink in. And when they did, Devin's heart plummeted.

She didn't know why she was disappointed. She shouldn't have even been surprised. "Is this some trumped-up scare tactic to get me to drop the guardianship case?"

His eyes narrowed. "No."

"Has Steve really found something in the will?"

"Devin—"

"I don't believe you." Why, oh, why did she keep letting her guard down? What was the matter with her?

"Believe me," Lucas stated, voice hard as steel, "Steve has found something. And if you and I duke it out in court, Amelia will be the loser. Your testimony, misguided as it is, will play right into his hands."

"I am *not* giving up on guardianship of Amelia." She flattened herself against the pool wall, hands sloshing through the tepid water as she stepped sideways toward the ladder. "This conversation is over."

He reached out and gasped her wet arm. "I'm not asking you to give up on guardianship, Devin. I'm asking you to buy us time for Amelia's sake."

She shook off his hold, fighting the tingle that was left behind from his fingertips. "You've never done a single thing for Amelia's sake."

"You don't know that."

"Yes, I do." She rubbed the arm where he'd touched her, fighting hard to ignore his closeness, the darkness around them, the cool water lapping against her bare skin.

"You won't even listen," he accused.

"I've been listening plenty. All I do is listen to you. And I give you the benefit of the doubt, over and over—"

"Ha!" he scoffed.

"And I make stupid decisions."

He moved in. "And you don't think I do? I make the stupidest decisions in the world when it comes to you." His body brushed up against hers, thigh-to-thigh, belly-to-belly.

"Lucas," she gasped, reacting instantly to his touch.

Her skin flushed hot, her nipples beaded, while raw desired pooled in the base of her belly.

In slow motion, he tipped his head, and she held her breath, waiting for his lips.

The peach-colored fabric for Devin's bra had gone translucent in the water, the image dancing through Lucas's brain. Her nipples were hard, and the filmy fabric revealed every nuance of her gorgeous breasts. Her face was red, her full lips parted.

With steely determination, he kept himself from completing the kiss. Instead, he slid his fingertips along her slick arm and rounded her shoulder, skimming his way to the curve of her neck.

Her pupils dilated, and her breath came in small gasps. He knew he was playing with fire.

The ripples from the water lapped between them. His hand slid around to the nape of her neck, fingers inching into her hairline as he urged her closer still.

"I can't trust you," she told him, even as she tipped her chin and canted her face to the right angle.

"I know," he responded softly, the words more a caress than part of a coherent conversation. But he understood her position. He didn't much care about it at this exact moment, but he understood it.

"And you can't trust me," she breathed, her words and her body giving him mixed messages.

He shifted so that their bare thighs brushed together. "I know that, too," he answered with honesty.

He gave in and brushed his lips against hers in a tender, painfully brief kiss. It was more a question than a statement. If she was going to back off, he needed her to do it now...right now.

Instead, her fingertips fluttered across his bare chest, sending spikes of desire deep into his belly.

"Stalemate all over again," she murmured.

"Story of our lives." And he kissed her harder, parting his lips, sliding his free hand around the base of her spine, dragging her into the cradle of his thighs, nothing but the thinnest silk separating her heat from his need.

"This won't—" The rest of her words were lost on a gasp, even as her arms twined around his neck, her plump breasts pressing against his skin, her hard nipples burning him like a brand.

He deepened the kiss, his tongue tangling with hers, while one hand smoothed her hair, caressed her neck, her cheek, brushed across her tiny ear. She was so perfect, so delectable, he couldn't kiss her enough, couldn't touch her enough, couldn't hold her tightly enough.

Her palms ran over his shoulders, sliding across his slick, wet skin, tracing the curve of his biceps, searing a train of heat wherever they went. He felt his muscles bunch to steel. Every inch of his body hardened, and his tunnel vision narrowed to Devin.

He kneaded the small of her back, slipping his fingertips under the elastic of her peach panties. The slippery sensations of skin, silk and water brought a groan from deep in his throat.

Her tongue answered his, and her hands grasped his shoulders, small fingers digging erotically into his tightening muscles. He cradled her bottom, lifting her easily, pulling her against him as she bobbed in the cool water. Her legs wrapped around his waist, and his body reflexively arched against hers. He cursed the fabric separating them.

She moaned his name, and he felt himself move to the ragged edge of control.

"Not here," he managed to say, but he kissed her longer and harder and deeper.

"Then—"

His hand closed over her pert breast, and she gasped out loud.

The stairs were only a few feet away. He could do this. He moved toward them.

Without breaking the kiss, he mounted the short staircase in the shallow end of the pool. He carried her across the deck, past the towel rack, snagging his running shorts before taking her into the dark warm depths and privacy of the pool house.

She drew back, blinking her glazed eyes before glancing at the daybed in the small, dimly lit room. She seemed to hesitate. "This is a bad—"

He strummed the pad of his thumb across her swollen nipple, and she sucked in a breath. Her thighs convulsively tightened around him, and he felt a shot of raw lust cascade through his body.

He already knew this was a bad idea.

It was a terribly stupid, reckless idea.

But he was far past caring.

He captured her mouth with his, kissing her deeper still. His hands slid over her satiny skin. He inhaled her scent, tasted the sweetness of her mouth, groaned in near ecstasy when her small hands stroked from his chest to his waist and below.

He sat back on the daybed, flicked the clasp of her bra, then tossed the delicate garment aside.

"You are gorgeous," he groaned, caressing her breasts all over again.

She tipped her head back, her eyes going shut, the apex of her body pressed tight against him. He rotated his pelvis, savoring the sensation. Her hands clasped his thighs, each fingertip a pinpoint of sensation.

He feathered a touch along her inner thigh, traced the edge of her filmy panties, slipping inside until she gasped and squirmed against him.

He caught her moan in a hot, deep kiss, while he stripped off his boxers, groping in his running shorts for the condom in the pocket.

He found it, but her panties were in the way.

He fisted his hand around one strip of lace. Cursing in frustration, he jerked the fabric and it easily tore away.

Devin wrapped her arms around his neck, pressing her gorgeous body against him, kissing his neck, his ear, his temple, running her hands through his hair and holding tight.

He bracketed her hips with both hands, slowly pushing his way inside her, inch by amazing inch, feeling her hot body clasp him. He bent his head and kissed one nipple, drawing it into the cavern of his mouth.

"Lucas," she cried, and he thrust all the way home.

Her lithe body molded around him, and instinct took over as he pressed and withdrew.

The hot summer air surrounded them. The scents from the garden swirled in. The glow of the yard lights seemed to dance through the window, while the sensations of Devin hijacked his brain.

She kissed him.

Deeply at first.

Then more gently, more slowly, as if she was savoring the sensations.

Her body matched his thrusts, her breathing deep and steady.

She cradled his face with her hands, drawing back ever so slightly, gazing into his eyes, hers glowing midnight, sparkling with blue diamonds.

He slowed the rhythm, while they stared at each other. Neither said a word, but their communication was finally clear, crystal clear, no pretense or posturing between them.

He tried to hang on.

He desperately wanted to stop time. Right here. Right now. Forever.

But instinct took over. His pace increased, and her eyes fluttered shut. She clung tighter, and he rose higher and higher until her cries pierced the summer dark, and he followed her over the edge.

His heart thundered. His lungs dragged in air, his body desperately trying to recover from their cataclysmic lovemaking.

Devin melted against him, her hot body obviously spent, sweat mixing with pool water on his slick skin, and he laid back on the daybed and hugged her to him. He stroked her wet hair, kissed her temple, smoothed his hands down her bare back.

"Hoo, boy," she breathed in his ear.

"You okay?" he asked softly.

She was silent for a long moment. "Define 'okay'?"

"I didn't hurt you?"

Her body quaked with a brief chuckle. "I'm not hurt. Surprised, maybe."

"You're surprised?" He drew back so that he could look into her eyes. "I saw that one coming a mile away."

She shook her head in denial, but he wasn't going to let it go that easily.

He caught her gaze once more. "Are you saying I'm the only one of us who's been fantasizing all week long?"

She glanced off to the side without answering.

"Admit it," he cajoled.

This time, she dropped her forehead against his. "There's something wrong with us."

"We're healthy adults?"

"We're making a bad situation even more complicated."

"Devin?"

"Yes?"

"It's okay to take a break here. We can easily restart the fight again tomorrow." Cradling the back of her neck, he gently laid her head against his shoulder. For the moment, he just wanted to hold her close. He wasn't ready to let go.

"Are you declaring a truce?" she asked, voice muffled.

"A truce is better than a stalemate," he sighed, settling her in the circle of his arms, burrowing his face into the crook of her neck and inhaling her fresh scent.

She relaxed against him, her lips brushing his hairline as she spoke. "Just until breakfast, okay?"

He kissed her neck, then he kissed her ear, then he drew back and kissed her swollen lips, once, then twice, then a third, long time. "Until breakfast," he agreed, feeling arousal pulse through his body all over again.

In the breakfast alcove off the Demarcos' big kitchen, Devin kept her attention studiously on Amelia in the high chair, spooning rice pablum into the baby's mouth, while various staff members worked in the kitchen.

Across the table, Lucas had long since finished an omelet and was sipping his second cup of coffee.

"Is that enough, sweetheart?" Devin asked as Amelia pursed her mouth against a spoonful of pablum.

Amelia kicked her feet in response and reached her hand out for the small bottle of apple juice sitting on the table. Devin swiftly wiped Amelia's mouth and handed her the colorful juice bottle.

"Is that the plan?" asked Lucas, voice flat.

Devin glanced around and realized the kitchen had emptied of staff.

"What plan?" she asked cheerfully, without meeting his eyes. Instead she mopped up the splashes of pablum from the high-chair tray before taking a bite of her toasted blueberry bagel that had long since gone cold.

"We pretend it never happened?"

"I like it." Devin nodded and wiped the high-chair tray with the damp cloth. "It's a pretty good plan."

In the cold light of day, she couldn't believe she'd had sex with Lucas, in the pool house, with bohemian abandon.

She'd yelled.

She wasn't a yeller.

What had gotten into her? What must Lucas think?

"Look at me," he told her.

She didn't. "Why?"

"Are you embarrassed?"

"No." Not exactly. Okay, yeah, *embarrassed* would be a good word. She made sure the corners of the high-chair tray were spotless.

"Because there's nothing—"

"Lucas." At the end of her rope, she set down the cloth and glared at him. "Can we not talk about this?"

He paused, looking uncertain. "I just wanted to make sure you were okay."

"I'm fine. I'm great. I've got a lot to do today."

Amelia was running low on diapers and applesauce, and Devin was determined to get some writing done at nap time.

Lucas cleared his throat. "We still need to talk about Steve. We still need to talk about the nanny."

"I *do* have a life, you know."

He went silent for another moment. "I never said you didn't."

"It can't all be about your agenda."

"My *agenda* is to take care of Amelia."

"Well, so is mine."

"Good. Then we agree."

Amelia dropped her bottle on the hardwood floor, and Devin bent to retrieve it.

She sat upright again. "I doubt very much we agree on anything."

His eyes flared with determination. "We agreed last night."

Devin brought her hands down on the tabletop. "Are you going to throw last night up in my face forever."

"I meant we agreed to face the truth last night. And eight hours isn't forever?"

Amelia had grown tired of sitting in the high chair and started to squirm.

Devin reached over and untied her bib, folding the damp

fabric and placing it on the table. She squeezed the latch on the high chair tray and slid it forward, reaching under Amelia's arms to lift her out.

Lucas stood up. "You are completely rattled."

"No, I'm not." But she knew he was right. Last night had seemed like a good idea at the time. Okay, it had seemed like a great idea at the time, but now she realized that by sleeping with Lucas she had given him the advantage.

Because, while he seemed perfectly capable of casual sex, Devin found her feelings for him hopelessly confused. On the one hand, she wanted to fight him. She needed to keep fighting him for Amelia's sake. On the other hand, she found herself wanting to continue the truce.

Maybe she just wanted to sleep with him again. Or maybe she needed to convince herself that it was more than just lust last night. How could she enjoy sex so much with a man she didn't respect and admire? It didn't make sense.

Nothing made sense this morning.

A staff member entered the kitchen and began clearing up the coffee service from the breakfast bar.

Lucas dropped his voice. "We need to talk."

"We just did."

"We need to be together on this, Devin."

She tucked Amelia against her shoulder. "We need to forget it ever happened."

"I'm not talking about sex," he hissed, and the staff member faltered in her cleanup.

Devin frowned.

Lucas leaned closer. "Steve. We need to be together against Steve."

"Not now," said Devin with a shake of her head. She needed time to herself. She needed to get her head on straight about, well, everything.

"Then when?" he persisted.

"I don't know." She paused. "Tomorrow. Okay? Tomorrow."

"Devin." His exasperation was clear.

She moved toward the door to the main hallway. "Back off Lucas. I need a little time."

Seven

Lucas tracked Steve down to his executive office on the fifteenth floor of the Pacific Robotics building. It was nearly noon, and sunshine streamed through the floor-to-ceiling windows of the ultramodern, European-styled office.

The desk was stark white, plastic with rounded edges, no drawers and a Plexiglas top that reminded Lucas of a kid's toy. The chair matched, molded plastic with white vinyl cushions. While the white shelf unit behind Steve held numerous impressionist glass objects for which he'd likely paid a fortune.

His computer was a bright white flat screen with a sleek matching keyboard, there wasn't a single piece of paper in the office. The only splash of color was a metallic abstract painting, in aqua and silver on the side wall. Lucas was forced to squint against the glare.

"Lucas," Steve greeted with a smug, half smile as he swiveled his chair back and forth a few degrees. His suit was steel-gray, his dark hair stark against the white background.

The door firmly shut behind him, Lucas advanced on the desk. He folded his arms over his chest. "Just what the hell do you think you're doing?"

"At the moment, I'm composing a memo."

"You think you can intimidate Devin?"

Steve stopped swiveling and sat up straight. "I don't know what you're talking about."

"You don't think I'll protect her?"

Steve scoffed out a cold laugh. "I think you'll protect your investment."

"I can't believe you'd target a defenseless woman."

"Unlike you?" Steve sneered.

Lucas pointed sharply with his index finger. "I have never—"

"Never what? Never fought Devin Hartley for control of Amelia? Never conspired with Konrad to manipulate Granddad's will?"

"You *know* that's a lie."

"I know nothing of the sort."

"You better back the hell off on this one, Steve. I am not letting you anywhere near Devin and Amelia."

Steve laughed at that. "What are you, saddling up the white charger now? Galloping on over to the moral high ground? You'd have kicked Devin to the curb months ago if you'd been able to get away with it."

Lucas stilled, because Steve was right. If Lucas had found a way to get sole guardianship of Amelia, he wouldn't have given Devin another thought. But that was then. This was now. All he could seem to think about was Devin's welfare. And he was *not* going to let Steve hurt her.

Steve obviously sensed his advantage, because he came to his feet and his voice got louder. "You want Amelia because she gives you control of the company. So don't stand there and pretend this has anything to do with Devin."

Lucas leaned in. "You'd have her disinherited? You'd have Konrad's only child disinherited for your own selfish ends?"

"Like you wouldn't if it was my child."

"I wouldn't," Lucas answered honestly. Much as he'd hate Steve having control over Pacific Robotics, he would respect his grandfather's wishes.

"You lie almost as well as I do," Steve returned.

"I'm not going to let you do this," Lucas warned.

"You have absolutely no way to stop me," said Steve. Then he lifted his chin, a reptilian smile coming over his face. "The high-and-mighty Lucas Demarco, sidelined in his own company. I hope you weren't too fond of the corner office."

"You think *that's* what I'm fighting for? Status?" Lucas was fighting for the financial health of the company, the security of their employees, the interests of the Washington State high-tech sector and the future of his brother's baby girl.

"You are staid, complacent and unimaginative. If you had the capacity to even consider enlightened business practices, we wouldn't be having this conversation."

"Depriving a child of her inheritance is neither imaginative nor enlightened. It's criminal."

"What's criminal, Lucas, is having a baby for the sole purpose of financial benefit. You expect any judge to believe Konrad met his soul mate and fell in love forty-eight hours after we read Granddad's will? Or that normal people plan a five-hundred-guest wedding in less than a month? Or that, in this day and age of birth control, people get pregnant on their wedding night?"

Lucas didn't particularly want to present the facts that way to a judge. But, yes, he believed all of those things happened with Konrad and Monica. He watched his brother fall apart after she left. He watched Konrad try anything and everything to win her back.

There wasn't a single doubt in his mind that Konrad had loved both Monica and Amelia.

Steve plunked back down in his chair. "She left him, Lucas. She knew she'd been used. Her sister knows the truth. You're the only one persisting in this fairy tale."

"I don't want you anywhere near the mansion," Lucas intoned. "I don't want you anywhere near Devin. And I especially don't want you anywhere near Amelia."

"I don't have to go anywhere near them," Steve returned. "The facts will speak for themselves. I honestly don't know why I didn't think of this earlier." His eyes narrowed. "I'm going to win this, Lucas. I'm going to win this because you have never been able to see the potential in any circumstance. You're not

Konrad. You'll plod along the safe road, following the rules, keeping everything inside the lines." He paused, curving the corners of his mouth into a slick smile. "Did I tell you I'm engaged? Wonderful little woman I've been seeing for nearly six months. Expect a wedding invitation. We're planning a big family."

Lucas swore out loud.

"Yeah," Steve said, grinning. "It is, isn't it?"

"It wasn't exactly the worst mistake in the world," Lexi offered from where she'd stretched out on her stomach on the blanket they'd spread on the rolling lawn in the backyard of the Demarco estate. They were up the hill from the mansion, close to an oriental garden where one of the young housekeepers named Teresa was helping Amelia feed the koi fish.

Amelia was delighted by the fish. She especially loved standing on the small stone bridge, clinging to the rail and staring down at their flashing colors. Teresa seemed endlessly patient with her, and delighted to be asked to help out. Today Devin was inclined to take advantage of the young woman's assistance.

"So, it's the second-worst mistake?" asked Devin, plucking a blade of grass from the lush lawn. She sat cross-legged on the bright blue blanket, gazing past the gardens to Puget Sound and the ships gliding past. If sleeping with Lucas came second, she'd hate to think about what was first.

"Do you think it was part of his grand scheme?" asked Lexi.

"*I* was the one who was supposed to use sex to learn *his* secrets." Devin shook her head now when she thought back to that ridiculous plan.

"You told him secrets?" Lexi's interest perked up a notch.

"I don't have any secrets."

"Does he?"

"I don't know." Devin tore the blade of grass lengthwise. "I think he does. He knows perfectly well that Konrad used

Monica for his own financial ends. I'm sure Lucas was part of the plot."

Devin hadn't yet decided what to do about Lucas's request that she postpone the hearing. It could be another scam. Then again, she could easily believe that Steve was up to no good.

"I thought you were only going to dress up and give him a few 'come hither' looks?" Lexi reminded her.

Devin felt her face heat with embarrassment. Could she have done a worse job with it? "I was in jogging shorts. Well, okay, my underwear."

Lexi sat up, eyes alight. "You were vamping him in your underwear? And you wonder why things went off the rails?"

"I was swimming in my underwear. And we were arguing. I wasn't vamping. That's why I didn't expect…"

"Okay, back to the underwear part in just a second. What I don't understand is why you said yes."

Excellent question. Devin wished there was a noble answer. She rolled, aimed and tossed the blade of grass onto the lawn, merely postponing the inevitable admission. "He's hot. And he's a great kisser."

Amelia squealed in delight in the distance, while Lexi just grinned. "So, there was an upside to this."

Devin gave a sheepish grimace. "If you mean great sex, then yeah. There's an upside. But there's a humongous downside too."

"It doesn't really change anything," Lexi pointed out.

"It's *embarrassing.*" Devin had to spend the next month with Lucas, and he'd seen her naked.

And she wanted to do it again. And she was terrified that he'd figure that out.

No good could come of a distracting affair with Lucas. She needed to keep her wits about her.

Beside the koi pond, Teresa held on to both of Amelia's hands while Amelia began walking their way.

"So, what now?" asked Lexi, flicking her hair over her shoulder and readjusting her position on the blanket.

"I still need a plan. I need to prove beyond any doubt that

Konrad and Lucas plotted the romance with Monica to get the inheritance."

"How're you going to do that?"

"Wait until he's out of the house, and then snoop around. I'll hunt for evidence. Talk to witnesses."

Lexi straightened. "Can I help?"

"Absolutely."

"When do we start?"

Devin came up on her knees and moved closer to Lexi so she could lower her voice. "Today." She nodded archly. "I'm going to let Teresa put Amelia down for her nap. Lucas is going into the office for the afternoon. And I need you to distract Byron."

Lexi frowned. "I really don't like that man."

"I didn't ask you to like him."

"He's smug. That 'y'all' and 'ma'am', and the slow talkin' drawl. It's an act. He's devious."

"All the more reason to keep him distracted for me." Devin wasn't sure she'd call Byron devious. But she'd definitely bet he was more intelligent than he let on. And he seemed intensely loyal to Lucas.

He'd talked yesterday about heading home to Texas. But he was still here. And Devin couldn't afford to wait.

Lexi squared her shoulders. "Where is he now?"

Devin tilted her head. "Over at the pool. Put on your turquoise bathing suit and go out on the floatie again. He seemed to like that."

"Are you my pimp?"

"Do it for Amelia," Devin cajoled.

Lexi drew a breath. "Okay. Fine. For the sake of our baby princess, I'll let the man ogle me for a while." She rose to her knees. "I just hope that ostentatious belt buckle of his doesn't catch the sunlight and blind me forever."

"Drama queen," breathed Devin.

"Hey, you're not the one who'll be using sex to…" Lexi paused. "Wait a minute—"

"Shut up," said Devin.

Lexi laughed at Devin's outrage. Then she sobered. "Okay."

She smoothed back her hair. "I'll vamp the tall cowboy. You snoop around inside the house. Someday, this is going to make a funny story for Amelia."

With Amelia safely down for her nap, and Lexi running interference with Byron down at the pool, and Lucas gone to the office, Devin crept into Konrad's silent bedroom.

It was an opulent suite on the north wing of the second floor, down the hall from Lucas. Elaborate gold and cream ceilings blended into crown molding that outlined the L-shaped room. A huge, four-poster bed was set into the alcove. A sitting area was formed by four brown leather, overstuffed armchairs that surrounded a marble fireplace and two antique, glass-topped tables. Three bay windows brought sunshine in from the ocean side, while a boxed window above the king-size bed overlooked the pool.

The thick carpet was soft under her canvas runners, and she found her gaze drawn to three massive seascapes hanging on the pale yellow walls. The scenes were calm and soothing, with whispery grasses and delicate wildflowers blooming along the shores. It wasn't what she would have expected of Konrad.

Taking a bracing breath, and telling herself she had no choice but to snoop, she started with a small desk in one corner, carefully and quietly pulling open the three drawers. The contents were impersonal—a pad of paper, a few gold pens, a phone book and a calculator.

Next, she moved to one of the dressers, wiping her damp palms across her blue jeans before flipping up the iron handles and pulling open the top drawer. It was Konrad's underwear. Though she herself kept many precious bits and pieces in her underwear drawer, she wasn't going there. There might be a signed confession hidden beneath his boxers, but she wasn't willing to dig it out.

The remaining dresser drawers mostly held T-shirts, sweatpants and pajamas. She closed them up and moved to the closet.

There she was shocked to find some of Monica's clothes still hanging in neat rows and folded on banks of shelves. At least Devin assumed they were Monica's clothes. They were about the right size, and it was definitely Monica's wedding dress hanging in the far corner, covered in plastic film.

For a moment, Devin's throat closed up with loneliness. She took a few steps closer and reached out to touch the dress.

It had been such a blissful wedding, full of excitement and promise. It was the most elegant event Devin had ever attended and, at the time, she'd fully expected Monica to live happily ever after.

Monica had been radiant, and Devin herself had felt incredibly beautiful that night. She'd worn a floor-length, violet silk dress, with a spray of flowers in her hair, and a delicate diamond pendant that Monica had given her as a bridesmaid gift. She'd danced with other guests until her feet were blistered, toasted the bride with expensive champagne, nibbled on crab puffs and ate two pieces of cake.

Later, when Monica walked out on Konrad, they'd trashed her bridesmaid dress and thrown out the pictures. But Devin hadn't had the heart to get rid of the pendant.

Her sister's veil hung next to the white silk dress. The shoes on a bottom shelf. And above the shoes…

Devin crouched down. She stared intently before running her fingertips over the smooth white cover of their wedding photo album.

It had been a year since she'd seen any of the wedding pictures. After only a moment's hesitation, she slipped the album from the shelf and sat fully down on the thick carpet. With a deep breath, she opened the cover.

Monica was on the first page, standing alone in her wedding dress, silhouetted against the arched oak door of the stone church building. The dress was a masterpiece, several thousand seed pearls sewn into a strapless bodice with a sweetheart neckline and a full skirt, all accented with antique lace. They'd ordered it from a famous designer in Italy. Monica had balked at the price, but Konrad had insisted.

A tear slipped from Devin's eye as she turned the page. There, she saw Konrad, looking sharp in his tux. She struggled to work up some anger toward him, but all she could remember was how she and Monica laughed over a groom who owned not one, but half a dozen tuxedos. What kind of a man required half a dozen tuxes?

The next page showed Monica, Devin and the other bridesmaids—two of Monica's college roommates. They were laughing as they displayed their bouquets of irises and white roses. The photo had been taken moments before they moved from the anteroom to the foyer of the church. On the way down the narrow hallway, Monica had nearly caused a disaster, tripping on the hem of her elaborate dress and stumbling into Devin.

Fortunately, Devin caught Monica, the bouquets survived and the wedding guests hadn't heard their burst of laughter.

Devin swiped another tear from her cheek.

Next, she came to a picture of the wedding cake. It was a decadently rich, lemon-butter pound cake, six round tiers with white Belgian chocolate ganache. A pale gold luster adorned the icing, while a colorful waterfall of fresh flowers swirled diagonally down from a top bouquet. Devin got hungry just looking at it.

She flipped another page and came to Lucas.

"*What* are you doing in here?" his voice demanded.

Devin nearly dropped the album in shock. Her gaze flew to the closet entrance to see him looming over her, dressed in a business suit instead of a tux, frowning and furious instead of smiling for the camera.

"Don't *do* that," she cried. "You scared me half to death."

"What are you doing in here?" he repeated, eyes narrowing in suspicion.

Guilt and alarm invaded her system. "I…uh…" She swallowed over a sandpaper throat. What could she say? How could she possibly explain the fact that she was sitting on the floor of Konrad's closet?

"I got lost," she told him in a small voice, sticking to the only story she'd crafted. Then she glanced at the album, holding it up

as if it proved something. "I happened to spot this, and then...
well, I started looking, and remembering." She made a show
of swiping her cheek with the back of her hand, hoping for the
sympathy vote she supposed, since her excuse was transparently
lame.

Lucas took a couple of steps into the closet.

"You got lost?" he challenged, the skepticism all but dripping
from his tone.

"I, uh, took a wrong turn." She couldn't quite meet his eyes.
"Out there in the hall. This is a really big house."

She told herself to shut up.

His answering silence was unnerving.

After a long moment, he crouched down beside her. He
cocked his head to peer at the picture on the open page.

"You looked very handsome at the wedding," she offered,
pointing to his image. Truth was, he'd looked amazing that night
and every other time she'd seen him, including now.

She'd tried, but she hadn't come close to banishing her
memories of last night in the pool house. He'd looked amazing
then, too.

"Are you trying to distract me?" he asked.

"Of course not," she lied.

He reached out and tucked her hair behind one ear, letting his
hand rest there. "Then you're saying you find me attractive?"

"Yeess," she offered slowly, beginning to worry where he
thought this might be leading.

He ran the pad of his thumb from her cheekbone to the shell
of her ear, and along her jawbone.

Her pulse jumped at the intimacy of the touch. But she forced
herself to keep still, torn between trepidation and arousal, with
only one tiny, sane part of her brain reminding her she had to
put a stop to this.

She reached up and grasped his wrist, attempting to tug his
hand away.

She failed.

A lazy smile grew on his face, and his breath puffed sweetly
against her cheek, even as his thumb meandered to the curve

of her neck. "I can't help wondering." He paused. "Just how far you'd be willing to go to keep me distracted."

She swallowed again, her heart thudding deep in her tightening chest. "Why…" Her voice was a rasp. "Why would I need to keep you distracted?"

He leaned closer. "Because you're up to no good."

She bristled. "I told you. I got lost." But the lie sounded even worse this time around.

"And you accidentally wandered into Konrad's closet?"

"That's right." It could have happened.

"You're damn lucky I have a forgiving nature."

"Ha," she managed to scoff.

He sat down on the carpet beside her and lifted the album from her hands. "I've already forgiven you."

"I didn't do anything."

"Then why is your neck going all red and splotchy?"

Devin's hand automatically rose to cover it up, and Lucas grinned at the telltale action.

Then he shook his head. "I just hope I never need you to lie for me."

"That seems unlikely," she sniffed.

Instead of pressing further, he turned a page of the album. "You were very beautiful," he told her.

Devin turned her attention to a photo of her and Monica. "We threw out our pictures," she admitted.

"Yeah?"

She nodded. "We chucked my bridesmaid dress, too."

"She must have been pretty mad." He turned to a page that showed the bride and groom cutting the cake. Their smiles seemed so sincere.

"Can you blame her?" Devin asked.

"She made a terrible mistake."

"By marrying Konrad."

Lucas butted Devin with his shoulder. "Yeah, that's what I meant."

Devin gave a shrug. "You might have decided to finally be honest."

He shook his head in disbelief, folding the album shut and replacing it on the shelf.

Then, to her surprise, his hand slipped around to the back of her neck. His palm was warm, his gaze intent, and his voice sent a predictable quiver through the pit of her stomach. "You have got to be the most exasperating woman on the planet."

She struggled to hold on to her equilibrium, keeping her tone tart. "What? The women you know don't usually talk back?"

His lips relaxed to a half smile, and he leaned meaningfully toward her. "At this point, they usually stop talking altogether."

"Is that how you like it?"

"It makes the kissing easier."

"Don't you dare."

He grinned. "Why not?"

"Because you promised."

"I didn't promise a thing."

She ordered herself to stay strong. "Have a little respect."

"For what?"

"For this—" she gestured around them, hushing her voice in reverence "—for where we are."

"We're in my brother's closet."

"Exactly."

"You've never made love in a closet?" He was moving closer.

Of course she hadn't. She put her palm flat against his chest to hold him off. "Have *you?*"

"Not that I recall."

"You're joking, right?" How could a person not recall something like that?

"It's a pretty roomy closet," he pointed out, ignoring her question and making a show of testing the softness of the carpet.

"The truce is over," she reminded him, eyeing the closet door. She was sure she could make an escape. And she was positive it was the right thing to do.

"I'm willing to renegotiate," he told her.

"Lucas, be serious."

"What makes you think I'm joking?"

"I'm saying no."

He clamped his jaw. But he let his hand fall away. And he rose to his feet, holding out a hand. "Then, let's go."

She was glad he'd back off. She really was.

She stuck her hand in his and let him pull her to her feet. He kept hold of it, tugging her out of the closet and across Konrad's bedroom, through the open door to the hallway.

"Just so you know," he warned her as he pulled it shut behind them, "this room will have a lock on it from now on."

Eight

Devin couldn't pick locks, so Konrad's room was out of the question. But, she figured there were two people involved in this conspiracy. And if Lucas felt it necessary to lock Konrad's door, that meant there was something for Devin to find. If there was something to find in Konrad's room, there might also be something to find in Lucas's room the next day. So, the next day she set another plan in motion.

There were only a couple of weeks until the custody hearing, and she hadn't found anything in the rest of the house. Staff were either loyal to Konrad, or they had genuinely loved the man. Nobody had a bad word to say, and they all seemed to think Monica had been happy back then.

Devin waited until Lucas had left the mansion, and until Lexi, her stalwart partner in crime, had Byron's attention again at the pool. He'd put on a bathing suit today and joined her in the water. Devin was sure she'd get an earful about that from Lexi later tonight.

But, for now, she had Lucas's room in her crosshairs. Teresa turned out to be a godsend. She'd offered to take Amelia out in her stroller, up to the stable area where they could watch the horses. Amelia seemed fascinated by anything that moved.

The hallway was quiet outside Lucas's room.

Devin gingerly grasped the door handle, holding her breath

as she gave it a turn. But the mechanism clicked, and the latch gave way. The wide door swung open in front of her.

She gazed inside his inner sanctum, squelching the surge of guilt that washed through her stomach. This was even harder than it had been yesterday in Konrad's room. But there might be evidence in here that could help Amelia.

She forced herself to take a giant step inside. She pushed the door firmly shut, hearing the latch click back into place. Then she leaned back against the cool, solid wood while she gazed around the room.

It was rectangular. The ceiling was high, and the windows numerous, giving the room a light, airy feel. Leafy, dark green plants bracketed a set of glass doors that led to a balcony. A cream-colored sofa provided a centerpiece to a sitting area. The floor was polished maple, while the curtains and bedding shimmered with gold and emerald-green threads.

Devin was surprised to find the pale green wall panels lined with family portraits. For a few minutes, her attention was distracted as she peered at an old photo of a couple who were obviously Lucas and Konrad's parents. There were photos of Lucas and Konrad as young boys, and one of an older man that she strongly suspected was the grandfather who'd willed Amelia his shares in the company.

There was a portrait of Konrad and Monica that Devin had never seen. Monica was sitting in an elegant chair, wearing a low-cut, frosted pink, satin evening gown. Konrad stood behind her, a hand on her shoulder. He wore a tux with a pocket kerchief that matched the dress. It took a confident man to pull off pink satin.

Devin couldn't help wondering why they'd dressed up. Was it a party? One of the charity balls? Had Konrad written a large check that night to a worthy cause? Monica would have liked that about the Demarco family.

Devin found her fingertips going to the picture. They did look happy in this. It occurred to her for the first time that Konrad might have fooled Lucas along with everyone else.

But then she remembered the conversation her sister had

overheard. There'd been no doubt that Lucas was aware of Konrad's plot to get Monica pregnant. He'd called it brilliant, laughed at how they'd thwarted their cousin Steve. Not that Devin blamed them for wanting to thwart cousin Steve. But they didn't get to do it at the expense of Monica or any other unsuspecting woman.

Her gaze caught a photo of Konrad and Amelia. He was dressed casually, in jeans and T-shirt and, unlike the posed pictures, he was obviously unaware of the camera. Baby Amelia was asleep in her father's arms, her little hand wrapped around his index finger, mouth pursed and eyes closed. The expression of reverence on Konrad's face told Devin that he'd loved Amelia. Dearly.

Devin armed herself against the unexpected onslaught of emotion. Konrad loving Amelia didn't change the current circumstances.

Next to the picture, in a bay-windowed alcove, she spotted a computer sitting on a small desk and immediately she realized the potential. The brothers could easily have communicated by email. And, here in his bedroom, Lucas might not have protected his computer with a password.

If the messages went back far enough, she might find exactly what she was looking for.

She quickly sat down at the desk, swiveled the chair and pressed a key.

The screen came to life, and it was already on Lucas's email account.

Devin's heart thudded in excitement, and she rubbed her hands together. She scrolled down his folder list, easily finding a directory called Konrad. She clicked it and found hundreds of messages. It was a gold mine.

All she had to do was find the right date range, the time when Konrad first met Monica. Once there, she found a message labeled "date." It seemed promising, so she double-clicked to open it.

Remember that girl? the text read. I'll be late tonight. You're going to love her.

Devin sat back.

The girl was likely Monica. And Lucas was going to love her because she was the perfect patsy.

Devin opened the response from Lucas.

Go for it, this one read. Remember, I'm counting on you.

That was it. The smoking gun. Lucas was counting on Konrad to con Monica into marrying him and having his baby.

Devin opened the next message in the thread.

Start without me, Konrad had written. I'm staying until she kicks me out.

Start without him? What did that mean?

Devin glanced around for a printer, knowing she needed to print a copy of these. There it was. On top of a wooden file cabinet. She left the computer to turn it on.

Then she returned, clicking the final message in the thread that was labeled "date."

The Legion called about the estate was Lucas's response. They're thrilled to help with the scholarship. God, I miss him already.

Devin blinked. Scholarship? Legion? Lucas had to be talking about his grandfather's estate. They'd obviously set up—

A sick feeling hit Devin square in the pit of her stomach, and she staggered to her feet, backing away from the computer.

What was the matter with her? She was sitting here reading Lucas's private mail. No matter what the justification, her behavior was appalling. She couldn't do this. She couldn't use this information.

"—ready to head back in ten minutes," Lucas's voice sounded from the hallway.

Pure panic engulfed Devin.

She was about to be caught. Again. By Lucas.

She glanced wildly around the big room, searching for somewhere to hide.

"I'll meet you out front," Lucas continued, his voice closer now.

Devin's ears rang, her heart contracted and sweat burst out on her palms. Seconds from now he was going to walk in and catch her invading his privacy. She had no explanation, no defense. He'd be furious, and he'd be right.

The big four-poster bed had her trapped. It blocked her path to the closet, to the bathroom, even to where she could duck behind the couch.

In a split-second decision, she leaped to the bed, laid back on the pillows and crossed her bare legs in front of her.

Lucas opened the door and froze.

"Hi, there," she breathed. She batted her lashes in what she hoped was a come hither expression.

"What the…"

"I heard you come in," she bluffed, hoping against hope that it wouldn't twig on him she was dressed in a cotton tank top and shorts, hardly an outfit designed for seduction.

"Devin?" His gaze darted curiously around the room.

"Amelia's with Teresa," she continued. "And, I thought…" She let her voice trail off meaningfully, patting the bed beside her, hoping she didn't look like a complete idiot.

She'd never done anything remotely like this before in her life. And she was mortified to be doing it now. She smoothed back her hair and moistened her lips.

Lucas shut the door behind himself, taking a few steps forward. "I don't understand."

"I missed you," she lied.

"I've only been gone an hour."

"I mean, I *missed* you." She slid one bare leg up against the other, pointing her toe.

"Are you all right?"

Okay, she was starting to get insulted here. "Am I not doing this right?"

"Depends on what you're doing."

She held her palms out to the sides. "Grab a clue."

He moved closer still, cocking his head while he considered her. "Let me see. You're in my bedroom. You're lying on my bed. You're telling me the baby is otherwise occupied."

"Gold star so far."

He stopped at the edge of the bed. "Devin, are you trying to seduce me?"

"I'm obviously not doing it well." She told her ego to get over it. She didn't want to succeed here. She wanted to fail.

She wanted him to politely tell her he had work to do and he'd see her later. At which time, she would be completely occupied with Amelia. Or maybe she'd go out. Maybe she'd stay out all night, or at least late enough that he'd have to be asleep before she showed up.

"You're doing just fine," he told her. "I'm surprised is all."

"Good," she lied, forcing herself to relax as she gave him another bright smile.

He perched on the edge of the bed. "Was this a spontaneous decision?"

"Yes," she answered honestly.

He reached out to smooth back her hair. "You heard me come home and thought I'd like to…?"

His touch sent a lightning bolt of sexual charged energy down the length of her body. She sat up straight. "If you're too busy—"

"I'm not too busy." He shrugged out of his jacket.

Devin swallowed. "I mean, you know, this probably isn't the best—"

"Second thoughts?" He loosened his tie.

"No. Of course not. I, uh, want this." Oh, no. What now?

"I want it, too," he told her huskily, tossing the tie and stretching out beside her on the bed.

"Lucas—"

He pulled her down, wrapping her in his arms, looking straight into her eyes. "It's a very nice surprise," he told her. Then he dipped his head, and his lips touched hers, and her body ignited with white-hot arousal.

His arm wrapped around the small of her back, tugging her body against his own. Her lips automatically parted, and his kiss seemed achingly familiar. In the dim recesses of her mind, she knew she had to bring this to a halt. But reason quickly disappeared, and she wrapped her arms around his neck, surrendering to passion.

His hand slipped beneath the hem of her tank top, trailing up her side, his palm surrounding her breast. Her nipple peaked beneath his touch, and her body reflexively arched against him.

He stripped her shirt over her head and feasted his eyes on her white bra. His gaze was searing, taking in every inch of her body, while his hand went to the button on his dress shirt.

After a moment's fumbling, he swore beneath his breath and ripped off the buttons, tugging off his shirt. Her bra went next, and they were skin-to-skin, kissing their way to another plane of desire.

She found her hands going to his belt, releasing the buckle, popping the button, pulling down the zipper, even while his kisses roamed from her mouth to her neck and down to the peaks of her breasts. He stripped off her shorts in a heartbeat, then dispatched the rest of his clothes.

Again, they were skin-to-skin, with nothing between them. The world outside his bedroom, his bed, his hands and his lips ceased to exist. Devin longed to get closer, to press harder, to wrap herself around his magnificent body and travel to paradise all over again.

"You amaze me," he rasped, both hands cradling her face as he planted long, wet kisses on her swollen mouth.

She shifted her body, moving beneath him, kissing him hard and deep in return. She lifted her knees, wrapping herself around his hips, gasping his name as primal urges swept through her, robbing her breath and curling her toes.

His hand slid down her body, over the curve of her waist, across her hip, cupping her buttocks, and tugging her to him. He thrust, and she gasped, groaning in relief at the exquisite sensation of becoming one. A buzzing started in her ears, obliterating everything but Lucas's voice.

He told her she was beautiful, that she was amazing, that he'd never felt this way before, and that he never wanted to let her go.

The buzzing moved through her body, from her abdomen, to her breasts, to her thighs and to her toes.

His rhythm increased, and she arched her back. His hand found her breast, and sensation nearly blinded her.

She felt his muscles clench to steel, and she curled her body around him, hanging on tight and letting wave upon wave of pure released wash over her.

It was long minutes before her breathing slowed down.

Lucas was a hot weight on top of her, and she felt cocooned between him and the pillow-topped bed.

His hand stroked her face, and he gently kissed her temple, her cheekbone and the corner of her eye.

"I'm late," he told her, the regret in his tone convincing enough to take the sting out of his words.

"I know," she said and gave him a nod.

She'd let it happen. She'd actually taken her bluff to its final conclusion. She wasn't sure how she felt about that. But it was probably better if he left right away. Both her brain and her emotions were a jumble of confusion.

"I have time for a shower," he said, and the next thing she knew, he was lifting her from the bed, setting her gently on her feet and guiding her to a huge marble bathroom.

The shower was magnificent, and so were Lucas's hands.

Feeling warm and fresh, and preposterously euphoric wrapped in a fluffy, white terry-cloth robe, it wasn't until Lucas left her in her own room to change that she realized they hadn't used birth control.

She gripped the nearest bedpost, did a quick calculation on her fingers and realized the risk was minimal.

With a sigh of intense relief, she slumped down on the bed, wrapping her arms around her body and hugging tight. What on earth was happening to her here?

Lucas awoke in his bed the next morning thinking about Devin. His business dinner had run late. He'd briefly considered knocking on her bedroom door after he'd come home, and climbing into her bed to hold her in his arms. But he wasn't sure if he'd be welcome. He wasn't at all sure what to make of yesterday.

Talk about a complete one-eighty.

When he'd caught her snooping around Konrad's room, he'd got the impression their physical relationship was going to be a one-time thing. He wasn't happy about that. Who would be happy about discovering such an amazingly passionate woman, only to have her snatched away?

But he was prepared to accept her decision. With everything going on around them, it wasn't fair to push her. He hoped they'd at least agreed to a postponement of the court battle, although Devin hadn't exactly said that out loud yet. But the court battle would one day come. And they'd be on opposite sides, and it would be bloody complicated if they were also lovers.

Lovers.

Lucas tossed back his quilt.

Was that what they were now? Did Devin intend for them to make love again? She must. It wasn't like they'd accidentally fallen into each other's arms yesterday. She'd obviously made a deliberate decision to seek him out.

In his bed.

He grinned at the memory, folding his hands behind his head and staring at the ornate ceiling above him. So, was the next move his? Maybe she'd expected him to show up in her room last night.

How would she feel about sleeping together with Amelia right next door? Silly question. Amelia was only nine months old. And the mansion staff was nothing if not professional and discrete.

He glanced at his clock and decided he had a couple of hours to spare. He'd shower, find Devin and see if he could get a sense of where this thing between them was going.

He vaulted out of bed, a spring in his step as he moved through the motions of his shower and shave, wondering as he did if he'd find her at the pool, or maybe they'd taken a walk to the gardens. Or maybe, if he was lucky, Amelia was with Teresa and Devin would be free for the next little while.

It was Wednesday, so Lucas selected his usual white dress shirt, buttoned the front and the cuffs and twisted his tie into place with practiced ease. Shrugging into his jacket, he passed the computer and hit a key to bring up his calendar. Maybe he could get away with spending the entire morning here at the mansion. He grinned to himself for the hundredth time. Maybe he was premature in putting on his suit.

His email program came up, and he reached for the mouse to shrink it out of the way. But then his gaze caught Konrad's name in the list of recently-viewed emails.

What on earth? Who would—

But then the date registered, and he recognized the text. He dropped down into the chair, noting three of Konrad's other emails had been recently opened.

Reality hit him like a ton of bricks.

He twisted his head to stare at the messy bed.

She hadn't been here to proposition him yesterday. She'd hadn't heard him come home early and been overcome with passion and desire. The woman had been caught red-handed, and she'd slept with him to cover it up!

And she had the gall to question *his* ethics?

Lucas continued to stare at the emails, bitter disappointment fueling his anger. He told himself that at least he knew where he stood. Unfortunately, it didn't make him feel any better.

He pushed back the chair and rose to his feet. Then he straightened his cuffs and collar and paced deliberately for the door.

Her room was empty as he passed it, and so was the nursery. There wasn't a soul in the foyer or the great room. He caught a glimpse of Teresa down the hall, but she took one look at his face and veered off into the library. She was alone, and that fact told Lucas that Amelia was with Devin.

It wasn't until he made it to the kitchen that he heard voices. They were coming from the breakfast alcove that overlooked the pool. Lexi's laughter. Good. Devin couldn't be far away.

But then Byron's voice responded. "It wouldn't have been so

bad." His tone was laced with a deep chuckle. "But the bull's name was Clementine."

Lucas came around the corner.

"You're making that up," Lexi accused from where she sat on one of the curved bench seats at the round table, but there was a distinct thread of laughter to her voice.

"I swear it's the truth," said Byron, as Lucas's entrance caught his attention. "Look, there's Lucas. Lucas can tell you—" Then Byron did a double take of Lucas's expression. "What's wrong?"

"Where's Devin?" Lucas reflexively glanced around the room, moving so he could see to the far end of the kitchen and peering past the window planters into the yard.

"Did something happen?" asked Byron, coming to his feet.

"She's out with Amelia," said Lexi, worriedly watching Lucas.

"Lucas?" Byron prompted.

"I need to talk to her," said Lucas. He was doing his best to keep his temper in check, but the more he thought about Devin's behavior, the angrier he became.

What kind of a woman broke in to a man's email account? What kind of a woman slept with a guy to cover her tracks? She was one amazing actress. He could have sworn—

"Mr. Demarco?" Teresa suddenly rushed breathlessly into the room, her feet slipping on the linoleum as she rounded the corner. She braced her hand against the counter. "Something's very wrong out there."

"With Devin?" Lucas automatically asked, fear pushing out his anger.

"Out where?" asked Byron.

"Out front," Teresa answered. "At the gate. There's a big crowd of people."

"Where's Devin?" Lucas was already heading for the hallway.

"I didn't see her." Teresa shook her head. "Not out front."

"What kind of a crowd?" asked Byron, he and Lexi on Lucas's heels as they all rushed down the hallway.

"They have cameras and microphones."

Reporters? What would bring reporters to the estate?

Lucas pulled out his phone, pressing the speed dial number for Theodore Vick, talking to Teresa while the line rang. "When's the last time you saw Devin?" he demanded as he crossed the foyer and yanked open the door.

"They went to the park, maybe an hour ago."

"What park?" Did the reporters have anything to do with Devin? Was she up to something more sinister than snooping through his private correspondence?

The young woman's eyes went wide, and her voice quavered. "Beside the marina. She took Amelia in the stroller."

"Some of those are the big guns," said Byron. "SNN, The Evening." He lengthened his stride alongside Lucas.

"What the hell?" Lucas shaded his eyes. He'd had plenty run-ins with the press in the past, and he had no desire to make tonight's evening news. At the same time, he needed to know what brought them here.

"I can go down there alone," Byron offered.

"No thanks," said Lucas, giving up on Theodore and making up his mind to take the bull by the horns.

If this was something Devin had cooked up...

If she'd somehow decided engaging the press would help her cause...

"It's Lucas Demarco," one of the reporters cried out as he approached, and nearly two dozen people crowded the driveway gate. Their lights came on, and they began clicking pictures through the bars, their TV cameras whirring.

Lucas scanned the crowd, recognizing a couple of legitimate news organizations amongst the tabloid reporters and the paparazzi.

A woman shoved a microphone between the bars. "What do you say to the accusations of fraud, leveled at you by—"

"She's got the *baby,*" someone else cried out, and attention immediately shifted from Lucas to the sidewalk across the street.

One look at Devin's stunned expression on the far sidewalk told Lucas she'd had nothing to do with calling the press. Which left only one other suspect. Steve.

Everyone rushed toward her and Amelia, who was sitting in a navy blue stroller.

Lucas swore out loud, plugged in the combination for the driveway gate and rushed outside with everyone else, Byron at his side.

"Ms. Hartley," demanded the woman with the microphone, while shutters clicked and cameras whirred, everyone jockeying for an angle. "How do you respond to the accusation that your sister—" the woman glanced at a notepad "—your sister Monica was complicit in an attempt to defraud the Foster family out of fifty million dollars?"

While Devin blinked like a deer caught in the headlights, Lucas and Byron elbowed their way through the crowd. Lucas grabbed hold of a man who was leaning in to take a picture of Amelia, snagging him by the collar and all but throwing him out of the way. Byron broke the man's fall and shoved him to one side.

Lucas swiftly snatched Amelia from the stroller and tucked her against his chest, obscuring her face with the lapel of his suit jacket. Then he grasped Devin's hand.

"Leave the stroller," he ordered, pasting her to his side and shouldering his way back through the crowd.

The reporters rushed alongside them, peppering them with questions and snapping pictures.

"Will there be a lawsuit?" shouted one.

"Do you expect any arrests?" came another.

"Has there been a DNA test?"

Lucas was beyond furious with his cousin.

He shoved Devin firmly inside the gate, where Lexi and several staff members had congregated. Then he rushed through the opening himself, and Byron followed with the stroller, filling the space behind Lucas and turning to block the way of any reporter who might be foolish enough to venture onto private property.

"What on earth?" Devin said breathlessly, craning her neck, even as Lucas kept her moving steadily forward toward the sanctity of the mansion.

"It was Steve," Lucas growled. He was still plenty angry with Devin, but that conversation would have to be put on hold for now.

Amelia pulled back and looked up at him. He braced himself for one of her crying jags, but wasn't willing to let go of her just yet.

"But, *why?*" asked Devin.

For some reason, Amelia didn't cry. She simply blinked curiously at Lucas as he carried her toward the front stairs.

He looked to Byron to get his assessment of Steve's behavior. "What does he gain?"

Byron shook his head, looking as confused as Lucas felt. "Publicly discrediting you is all I can see him getting out of this."

"It's not a jury decision or even a hearing," Lucas pointed out. "It's a technical question."

Whether Amelia was entitled to inherit would be decided by a family law judge in some little office in the bowels of the state judicial building. It wasn't like public opinion would factor into it.

"He could be targeting Pacific Robotic's board of directors," offered Byron. "Ramp up some kind of a scandal against you?"

"Does he think he can get me fired as president?"

"I don't understand," Devin said. "What's going on?" Then she glanced from Lucas to Amelia. "Do you want me to take her?"

"She's fine," he answered shortly. When the crowd of reporters rushed Amelia, his protective instincts had kicked in. She was safe now. And since she hadn't started crying, she was just fine right where she was.

The group trooped through the doorway and into the foyer,

and Lucas breathed a sigh of relief. He waited until the staff went back about their business and only Devin, Byron and Lexi remained.

"So, what happens now?" asked Lexi. Like Devin, her gaze kept darting to Amelia in Lucas's arms, as if she expected him to drop her.

Lucas looked to Byron. "I don't see confronting him." He'd already tried both reason and intimidation. And Steve wasn't going to suddenly develop a conscience.

"The boys'd know how to take care of it back home," Byron offered, stretching out his interlaced hands and letting his knuckles crack.

"An assault charge isn't going to help us," said Lucas, much as he'd love to take a swing at Steve right now. *What* was the man thinking, painting a target on both Devin and Amelia? How did he sleep at night?

"I don't see the press attention interfering with the legal decision," said Byron. "The judge is going to follow legislation and precedent. I doubt he'll even be reading *The Tattler*."

"So, Steve's master plan is to aggravate us?" asked Lucas.

Seattle was a small city, and Pacific Robotics was a prominent business. Lucas had been in the spotlight many times before, and he knew the paparazzi would hound all of them for many long days to come. There'd be nowhere to hide.

"It seems like that's the case," said Byron.

"That reporter," Devin began. "She asked if we expected arrests. What did that mean? Who would get arrested, and for what?"

Lucas avoided making eye contact with her. His instinct was to worry about her, but he had to stay angry. "The reporter was fishing. Steve dangled a story in front of them, and now they're digging for the details."

"I don't want Amelia on the front page." Devin seemed to instinctively shift closer to Amelia, who had relaxed and was now a soft, warm bundle against Lucas's chest.

"Neither do I." His tone was sharper than he intended, and Devin gave a slight cringe.

"But they can't get on the estate?" Lexi questioned.

"Lucas?" It was Theodore Vick, who was hustling into the front hall. "Sorry. I was out on the water. I've got two men at the front gate now."

"It's under control," Lucas told him. "At least for the moment." Then he answered Lexi's question. "They'd have a hard time getting on the estate. But it's not a fortress."

"I'll bring in some extra men," Theodore offered. "We've got the new lighting system installed at the back of the property, and Chad will make sure the dock is guarded around the clock."

Devin reached out for Amelia, but she stopped herself short, pulling back in obvious surprise. "She's asleep."

Lucas glanced down to see Amelia's closed eyes. Her cheeks were rosy and her pink mouth was relaxed, slightly opened as she breathed in and out.

Lexi stepped in. "Looks like Uncle Lucas doesn't scare her so much anymore."

Lucas knew he had to focus on security. They needed a plan to protect Amelia and thwart Steve. But for a brief second, he let the unfamiliar emotion flash through his chest. Amelia trusted him.

He silently vowed that he wasn't going to let her down.

"Can you increase the video surveillance?" he asked Theodore.

"Absolutely."

"What about long-lens cameras?"

"I can't give you any guarantees," said Theodore. "I can put on some extra guys, but there's a lot of fence line to cover, and you're open to the bay. It's probably best to stay inside as much as you can."

Devin's eyes narrowed in concern. "For how long?"

"A couple of weeks," Lucas admitted. "Maybe. They'll go away once we have a decision on Steve's challenge of Amelia's inheritance. Byron's trying to get more information on the timeframe."

"And are you going to hide in the house?" Devin asked Lucas.

He shook his head. "I don't care if they take pictures of me."

"Should Devin care?" asked Lexi.

It was Byron who answered. "Does she want a private life after this is over?"

Devin glanced around the circle. "So, I'm a prisoner?"

"Unless you want to leave Seattle," suggested Theodore. "It's a local story. I doubt it would follow you out of state."

Devin crossed her arms over her chest. "Unfortunately, I've been sentenced to stay here in this house."

"You want to leave?" asked Lucas, thinking that it might not be such a bad idea to get Devin and Amelia out of town and away from Steve.

"Of course I want to leave. I want to go home."

Theodore shook his head. "Your house is out of the question. There'll be reporters there, too."

The news obviously surprised Lexi. "Am I going to be ambushed when I get home?"

"You should stay here," Devin declared.

"You can all come on down to Texas," Byron offered.

Lucas scoffed at the idea.

But Byron widened his stance. "Ain't *nobody* getting their boots on my land."

"What?" Lexi mocked. "You gonna shoot 'em fer trespassin'?"

Byron didn't answer, but his expression said he just might.

"You couldn't—" Lexi paused "—really shoot them." She cocked her head as she peered at Byron. "Right?"

Byron offered nothing but a self-satisfied smile.

Theodore spoke. "It's not the worst idea in the world."

Lucas met his chief of security's eyes, mentally debating the pros and cons. Amelia and Devin would be well out of both Steve's and the any reporter's reach. And although Byron wouldn't literally shoot anyone who trespassed, he definitely had some hard-bitten ranch hands on the payroll who would dissuade anyone from bothering the residents of the ranch. Long lenses would never find them from the road.

And it would throw Steve a curveball. It would throw Steve

one heck of a curveball, which was exactly what Lucas needed right now. He'd been reacting to Steve's maneuvers for days on end. It was about time he took some action on his own.

"Fine," he said, nodding decisively. "We'll go to Texas."

Devin's jaw dropped open. "But—"

"I'm coming, too," Lexi immediately insisted.

"Isn't that a bit drastic?" asked Devin. "First I leave my home to come here, and now you want me to traipse halfway across the country?"

Lucas understood the reason for her reluctance. If she was in Texas, she couldn't snoop. There'd be no way for her to continue pawing through his private correspondence.

Too bad, honey.

They were *so* going to Texas.

Nine

Devin had never given any thought to the practicality of owning a private jet. But when they'd made the decision to head for Texas, they hadn't looked up schedules, they hadn't called a travel agent, Lucas had simply contacted his pilot to let him know they were going to Dallas.

They'd taken a helicopter from the estate to the airport, leaving reporters at the front gate unaware of who had left the estate and who was still inside. Not that anyone expected a reporter to follow them from Seattle to Dallas. Still, it was nice to know their journey was all but untraceable.

On the downside, Lucas had remained aloof throughout the trip and throughout the evening after they'd arrived. Devin wasn't sure what she'd expected. But after they'd made love a second time, and seemed to have come to a temporary truce, she hadn't expected him to use every excuse in the book to keep from speaking with her.

And it proved easy for him to keep his distance. Byron's homestead was more of a town that a house. Set on a grassy hillside a few hundred feet up from the picturesque Lake Hope, the complex consisted of a sprawling main house, with nearly a dozen other houses facing the lake. Two rows of smaller cottages sat farther up the hillside, and she was told they housed the ranch staff.

Teresa had come along to help with Amelia, while Devin

assumed Lexi simply wanted to avoid the reporters who seemed likely to have staked out Devin's house. The three women and Amelia were given rooms on the second floor of the main house, while Lucas had taken what he referred to as his usual house next door. Byron was in a massive master suite down the hall from the living room.

In true ranch style, the house was paneled in polished cedar, with hardwood floors, thick, patterned throw rugs and overstuffed leather furniture. The tables were pine, while the lamps bounced soft, yellow light to every corner of the rooms. The house's oil paintings had one theme—horses. Byron had ridden in rodeos in his late teens and twenties, and he had an obvious admiration for the animals.

This morning, Lexi had declared a desire to learn to ride, and the two of them had headed for the barns. Teresa had taken Amelia to check out the duck pond, while Lucas had announced he had phone calls to make back at his house.

Devin was left alone with her anger and frustration. Now that they were out of harm's way, she was furious with Steve. He'd thrown both her and Amelia to the wolves. They'd been defenseless against the press onslaught. Amelia's face was undoubtedly plastered in the newspapers, while Devin and Lucas's reputations would be dragged through the mud.

That wasn't even counting the physical danger he'd put Amelia in. She could have been trampled in the rush. Thank goodness Lucas had been there to save her.

Devin knew she should be working on her book. She even took out her laptop, settling herself in a corner of the living room, in a big comfy chair, with a warm breeze blowing through the screened windows against her bare arms and legs. But there were too many things on her mind. She simply couldn't focus on writing.

She wanted to rant about Steve. And she wanted to ask Lucas where he got off making sweet love to her one day, then pretending she wasn't even alive the next.

It wasn't as though they had nothing to discuss. They didn't have a nanny. And they were supposed to be united in fighting

Steve. Shouldn't they be strategizing? Maybe investigating? Information gathering? Filling out forms?

After an hour's frustration, Devin set aside her laptop and rose deliberately from the chair. She wasn't about to spend any more time in here sitting on her hands.

She stuffed her feet into a pair of sandals and straightened the short denim skirt that she'd paired with a violet tank top for the scorching summer day. Then she left through the front door, crossed a long porch and followed the wooden walkway that led to Lucas's house.

She knocked sharply, but there was no answer.

She waited, knocked again and finally decided to circle the house in search of him.

She followed a set of cement stepping stones that wound their way across the lawn. Once she cleared the building, she was rewarded. She heard Lucas's voice and tracked it over a small knoll, where she spotted him at the duck pond.

Dressed in blue jeans and a plain gray T-shirt, he sat on the ground, knees up, with Amelia clinging to his shoulder as a duck waddled toward the two of them.

Teresa was nowhere in sight.

Lucas tossed some crumbs, and the duck came closer.

Amelia squealed in delight, causing the duck to scoot away in fear.

She speed-crawled a few feet after it, and Devin found her steps slowing down to take in the astonishing sight. Lucas was playing with Amelia. They were all alone. And the two of them looked happy.

Something squeezed her heart. But she wasn't sure if it was joy or dismay. She'd have to admit Lucas would be the closest thing Amelia would ever have to a father. She shouldn't be anything but happy to see that relationship develop. Still, from an emotional standpoint, she loved Amelia so dearly, she didn't want to lose anything about her to Lucas.

While Devin watched, Amelia pushed herself to a wobbly standing position. Then she opened her hand and flung whatever she was holding at the duck. Devin couldn't tell from this vantage point if Lucas had given her bread crumbs or not. Apparently, neither could the duck. It waddled closer to investigate, fanning its wings and shaking its glossy green head while it scoured the ground.

Amelia made another throwing motion, then she turned to grin at Lucas, obviously seeking his approval.

"Clever girl," he cooed, with a deep threaded chuckle.

Amelia turned and took a step toward him, then another, and another. She walked until she was wrapped in Lucas's arms, laughing with pride at her accomplishment.

Devin swallowed a thick, burning emotion.

Amelia's first steps.

And they were to Lucas, not Devin.

Just then, he caught sight of her, and his expression sobered as he met her eyes.

Amelia wiggled out of his arms, and Devin pasted a bright smile on her face, crossing the remainder of the distance to the pair. Devin told herself there would be lots of steps in Amelia's life, and plenty of other firsts, and she intended to be around for all of them. And it wasn't as if she hadn't witnessed the first steps. She'd simply seen it from a distance, was all.

"She seems to like the ducks," Devin offered to break the silence.

Amelia crawled over and grabbed Devin's leg. Devin sat down so Amelia could get into her lap. The physical contact made her feel better.

"Where's Teresa?" she asked Lucas.

"She went riding."

"With Lexi and Byron?"

Lucas gazed off in the distance, while the ducks bustled around, searching for every last crumb. Sarcasm put an edge in his voice. "I don't think so."

Devin wasn't sure how to respond. The silence stretched.

Lucas finally spoke. "Byron and Lexi are on a date, and Teresa is checking out the cowboys more than she's checking out the horses."

"Byron's attracted to Lexi?" Devin had to admit, Lexi seemed less frustrated with Byron the past few days, but a date? That was a stretch.

"Lexi's a beautiful woman." There was a definite rebuke in Lucas's voice.

"I know that." Devin hadn't meant to imply she was surprised that Byron was attracted to Lexi. She loved Lexi, and Lucas was behaving like a jerk.

She watched the dozen ducks glide back out into the pond and decided it was best to change the subject.

"I came to ask you what's next," she told Lucas, helping Amelia to her feet as she held tight to her anger at Steve and her determination to support Amelia. She leaned back to balance on her arms, stretching her bare legs out in front. "Other than hiding out here, what do I do to help?"

He turned to gaze at her, anger coalescing in the pinpoints of his black pupils. "You can start by not reading my private emails."

The breath whooshed out of Devin, and a chill prickled her skin.

He knew.

He *knew*.

How on earth could she explain? "I didn't—"

"Didn't what?" he sneered. "Didn't break into my email account, or didn't have sex with me to cover it up?"

A pounding echoed in Devin's ears. Several of the ducks took flight, while Amelia tugged at a clump of grass.

"I have to admire your tenacity," he continued conversationally. "A lesser woman might have confessed she was spying, or maybe faked a headache, or just plain said no to sex, but not you, Devin, you stepped right on up—"

"Stop it!" She couldn't stand to hear him talking that way.

"Stop what? Stop telling the truth? Stop catching you in your little spy games?"

"I didn't…" She hesitated. What could she tell him? That she'd *wanted* to sleep with him a second time? That she'd missed his touch? That the minute he'd kissed her, she'd forgotten all about the emails and everything else in the world? Or maybe that she'd lain awake at night, having fantasies about the two of them making long, drawn-out, sexy love?

He'd never believe her. And she wouldn't want him to know. It would be beyond humiliating.

She straightened up, squared her shoulders and held her chin in the air. "Just tell me how I can help Amelia."

He glared a moment longer, but she firmly held her ground.

"You can help Amelia by not fighting me," he said.

"Fine," she agreed shortly.

"I need a letter, from you to the judge who's reviewing the will. I need you to support Amelia's legitimacy as Granddad's heir."

"In other words, you need me to lie. To a judge." She supposed it was always going to come down to this.

"No," he barked. "I need you to *stop* convincing yourself Konrad was dishonest. Quit looking for evidence that doesn't exist. He loved Amelia, and he loved Monica, and she broke his heart when she left him."

Was Devin simply supposed to ignore reality? "What about the corporate shares?" she demanded. "What about that conversation? What about Konrad telling you that he'd thwarted Steve by having Amelia?"

"Monica misunderstood."

"*That's* your story?"

"Did Monica love Konrad?"

The question took Devin by surprise.

Lucas spoke again, his voice staccato. "Don't lie to me, Devin. Did Monica love Konrad?"

"Yes," Devin admitted. She believed her sister had loved Konrad with all her heart. That's what made his betrayal so reprehensible.

Lucas's voice softened. "And how do you know that?"

"Because I know my sister. I lived with her through the whole thing. I saw what he did to her."

"And I know my brother. And I watched what it did to him. But that's a moot point. You need to write that Monica loved Konrad. Tell the judge they had a baby because they wanted to become parents. And tell him you have absolutely no evidence—"

Devin opened her mouth to rebut, but Lucas spoke overtop of her. "*No concrete evidence whatsoever,* that Konrad ever had any intention of duping Monica."

"What about the conversation?"

"Hearsay. You didn't hear it yourself, and Monica heard it out of context."

"That's a stretch."

"That's the truth. When she overheard our conversation, Konrad was being ironic. He told me marrying Monica to get her pregnant *would* have been the perfect plan. Not that it *had* been the perfect plan. We were laughing at Steve, not at Monica. Write that down."

"And then you'll have it on record."

Lucas's exasperated sigh was his answer.

"And when I fight you for Amelia, you use my letter against me?" It was a rhetorical question, and she didn't expect an answer.

"I can only solve one problem at a time," he stated, tossing a rock into the duck pond.

"Seems to me you're solving both of your problems in one fell swoop."

Lucas's gaze went to Amelia, who was now seated on the lawn, picking the heads off plump purple clover. "When she turns twenty-one, do you want to explain to her how we lost her inheritance?"

"No. But I also don't want to have to introduce myself to her."

Lucas rolled to his feet, jerking his hand in a gesture of frustration. "That is *never* going to happen. I won't keep you away from her."

Devin also came to her feet, straightening her skirt and brushing her backside. She wanted to believe him. She truly did. Her decision would be so much easier if she could trust Lucas.

"I'm supposed to believe you?" she challenged.

He took two paces toward her. "I'm not the one breaking into bedrooms and email accounts."

"You're also not the one taking a chance on my ethics. I'm taking a chance on yours."

"Well, thank goodness for that. Your track record so far is dismal."

Devin couldn't defend herself. He was right on that score.

The fight went out of her body, and the power went out of her voice. "I don't even know why I'm arguing with you."

Lucas drew back. His brows knit together in obvious confusion.

"I didn't come out here to fight," she told him. "I know who the real bad guy is." She pressed a hand against her forehead. "I came out here to ask you to annihilate Steve."

"Are you actually falling for Byron?" Devin stared at Lexi's sparkling eyes and flushed cheeks where she sat on the end of the bed in her ranch-house room. Lexi was fresh from a shower, wrapped in a thick white robe, drying her blond hair with a towel.

"It's a party," Lexi retorted. "He didn't invite me to a wild weekend in St. Kitts." Though her expression told Devin she'd probably consider a wild weekend in St. Kitts.

"You're flying all the way to Houston for a party?"

Lexi grinned. "*We're* flying all the way to Houston for a party. Byron wants all four of us to go."

"I can't go to Houston." Devin straightened on her perch at the other end of the bed. She was here to take care of Amelia, not to go gallivanting around the state of Texas.

"Don't be ridiculous." Lexi gave her a playful swat on the knee. "Teresa will take good care of Amelia. You need to do some research for your rich people book, and I need to take advantage of a date who owns his own jet plane."

"You are a mercenary," Devin playfully accused.

"He helped me get on my horse," said Lexi, biting down for a second on her bottom lip. "Then he helped me get off. And his hands lingered on my hips. I don't know why that seemed so incredibly sexy, but it did." She pressed the small towel into her lap, squeezing it between her palms. "I haven't kissed a man since Rick died. And we dated from the time I was fifteen, so I've never really kissed another man at all. I've certainly never made love to anyone else."

Devin blinked. "You're thinking about making love with Byron?"

Lexi's cheeks flushed brighter. "Maybe." She tossed the towel on the bed and finger-combed her long hair. "I don't know. I'm thinking about kissing him, anyway. Maybe tomorrow night at the party." She leaned forward, a pleading look in her eyes. "You have to come, Devin."

Devin wasn't crazy about the idea of flying to Houston. And she definitely wasn't wild about attending a party with Lucas.

She made an excuse to Lexi. "I don't have anything to wear."

Lexi grinned. "We'll go shopping."

"But—"

Lexi waved off Devin's protest. "Byron already told me I should go wild. We can stop in Dallas on the way, or we can make sure we get to Houston early. Come on, Devin. Designer dresses. Somebody else's credit card."

"Mercenary," Devin repeated.

"It'll be a blast."

Devin found she didn't have it in her to let Lexi down. It was the happiest she'd seen her friend since Rick had died. She'd buy a dress, make a little small talk and tough it out in Lucas's company.

It wasn't as though his opinion of her could get any worse. She groaned.

"What?" Lexi's voice betrayed her concern.

"Nothing." Devin shook her head. This was about Lexi. "I'll come to Houston."

"Is it Lucas?"

Devin's throat thickened for a split second, but she swallowed it away. "Of course it's Lucas. Everything is Lucas. My nemesis is Lucas."

"Because you hate him?"

"I don't hate him." She didn't. She hated the situation and the circumstances.

"Is it because you want him again, and you can't have him?"

Devin coughed on a exclamation of denial. "I don't want him."

Lexi lapped the robe over her thigh. "Uh-huh," she agreed sarcastically.

"And if I did," Devin declared, "I could have him any old time I wanted."

"Are you sure?"

"Yes, I'm sure. In fact, I already—" Devin stopped herself.

Lexi scooted eagerly up on her knees. "In fact, you already *what?*"

"Oh, hell." What was the point of pretending. "I did it again."

"Slept with Lucas?"

"Yes," Devin admitted.

"And you didn't tell me? When? Why? How?"

"How?"

"You know what I mean." Lexi wriggled closer.

"He caught me. Well, almost caught me. Snooping in his emails. I was looking for messages from Konrad."

Lexi gave an admiring nod. "Gutsy. I like it."

"I was in his bedroom." Devin couldn't help thinking back. "I heard him coming down the hall. So I hopped on his bed and acted like I was there to proposition him." She cringed at the memory.

"And he said yes?"

"Oh, yeah." A touch of pride crept into Devin's voice as she remembered Lucas's enthusiasm.

Lexi gave a throaty chuckle.

"But then, later, I guess the next day. I'm not sure. He found the emails, and now he thinks… Well, he thinks I'm the kind of person who'd use sex as a tool for covert operations."

"I think it's admirable."

Devin frowned. "That I'd use sex that way?"

"That you'd break into Lucas's email account."

Devin plucked at the quilt on the bed. "I couldn't do it. I mean, I know I did it. But I realized I'd gone way over the line. I was about to shut it down when he showed up."

She remembered the sick feeling in the pit of her stomach when she'd realized how badly she'd invaded Lucas's privacy. She was mortified by her own behavior, and she could certainly understand Lucas's disgust.

"I bet he would have done exactly the same thing," Lexi staunchly defended.

"You think?" Not that it gave her an excuse, but Devin would prefer to think she wasn't the only one whose ethics could be questionable.

"Don't let him paint himself as an angel. You're not perfect. Then again, neither am I. I'm thinking about sleeping with a man I only just met."

"Kind of like I did?"

Lexi reached out and squeezed Devin's hands. "We're human. It's not a flaw to be human." She paused. "So, what do you say about Houston?"

Lucas realized he was unlikely to ever see any of these people again. But he couldn't get past his discomfort at sitting in a pink armchair next to the lingerie section of Desmonde in downtown Houston, sipping a glass of white wine and pretending he cared about the fashion magazine the clerk had left open on his lap.

He tipped his body toward Byron and hissed. "We're shopping for *dresses*."

Byron leaned back in obvious self-satisfaction. "Do I know how to keep a little filly happy or what?"

"Can't we leave? And come back later?" Maybe they could find a sporting goods store or a cigar bar, somewhere Lucas could regenerate his testosterone.

"You've never been married, have you, Lucas?" Byron knew that perfectly well. "Trust me on this, I know what I'm doing."

"But I don't *want* to keep the little filly happy." Lucas plunked the magazine back down on the glass table in front of them.

He was willing to attend the party. It was a state board of trade event, so there were likely some good business contacts to be had. And Byron always supported Lucas, and Lucas understood Byron was interested in Lexi. But he didn't see why they had to traipse around Houston like a couple of college girlfriends, oohing and ahhing while Devin and Lexi chose dresses.

"Take a look at that," Byron cooed in a voice that carried across the room. "Isn't she the prettiest thing?"

Exiting the dressing room area, Lexi did an exaggerated model walk across the raised floor. The dress she wore was a brilliant blue, tight on top, with a full, layered crinoline-type skirt that fell to her knees. A jewel-studded belt flashed at her waist.

Lucas had to admit, Lexi had amazing legs for a forty-year-old.

Byron gave a low whistle, and Lexi flashed him a grin.

"Those shoes are a must," noted a salesclerk as she approached the dais.

Lexi turned her ankle to give them a better show of a pair of silver, high-heel sandals with wide ankle straps.

"You like the shoes, darlin'?" Byron asked.

"Love the shoes," said Lexi.

"We're taking the shoes," Byron informed the salesclerk. "And the dress. I'm particularly partial to the dress."

"It's the first one I've tried on," Lexi protested.

"Then try on some more," said Byron with a wave of his large, work-roughened hand. He lowered his voice to a conspiratorial level as he addressed the salesclerk. "Never known a woman to have too many dresses."

The salesclerk gave him a friendly pat on the shoulder, obviously sensing a hefty commission. "Neither have I," she readily agreed.

Devin appeared next, but Lucas barely got a glimpse of her black sheath of a cocktail dress before the salesclerk rushed to shoo her back into the change room.

Then the woman marched purposefully past Lucas to the lingerie, snagged a lacy black push-up bra and a scrap of a thong and whisked them toward the dressing rooms. "Nothing will ruin that Rue de Femme dress like panty lines," she announced to anyone who happened to be within earshot.

Lucas glanced uneasily at Bryon.

"Too much information," he finally responded.

"Way in the hell too much," Byron agreed.

Lucas shifted in his chair.

After a few minutes, Devin reemerged. The black dress was simple enough, a square neckline showing a creamy hint of cleavage, three-inch-wide shoulders straps that emphasized her slender arms, a nipped-in waist, clingy over the hips, narrowing to a hemline just above the knees. The dress wouldn't have normally stood out for Lucas. But Devin was wearing it, and all he could see was the image of that sexy underwear on what he knew to be a killer body.

The clerk stood back to consider. "That neckline simply cries out for diamonds," she commented.

The observation obviously took Devin aback. Her hand rose to her bare throat.

But Byron slapped one hand on his knee. "I'm buyin'," he announced in a hearty voice. "Bring on the diamonds."

"Like hell you are," Lucas retorted, while the clerk scurried off to the jewelry department.

"Nice shoes," said Byron, gesturing to the black suede platform sandals that were going to haunt Lucas's dreams.

"I'm not getting diamonds," Devin told them both.

Lucas lowered his voice so only Byron could hear. "And *you* are not buying Devin's underwear."

Byron slanted Lucas a look. "One too many roosters in the henhouse?"

"You want to buy underwear, buy some for Lexi."

The clerk hustled back to Devin, three velvet cases in her

hands. She opened the first, and the jewels flashed under the store lights.

"This one is called aurora swirl," she said. "Three-colored teardrop diamonds—blue, yellow and pink—with white square cuts in the chain—D flawless. And a total of seven carats in all."

Devin seemed speechless as the woman speedily fastened the necklace around her neck.

Byron leaned across the table separating them. "I suppose you'll insist on buying the diamonds, too?"

Lucas knew he should be annoyed at being backed into a corner, but he was too busy getting a kick out of the expression on Devin's face. He had to admit, the necklace looked stunning. The clerk knew exactly how to accessorize the dress.

"Let me get a better look," he said, motioning Devin forward.

The clerk smiled like a Cheshire cat, giving Devin a gentle little shove toward him.

Devin took a few halting tentative steps. Then she came down off the dais, her voice a low hiss. "Don't you dare encourage her."

"It looks good on you." Lucas spent only a fraction of a second on the diamonds before catching a glimpse of the lace bra peeking out above the neckline of the dress.

"Well, I think it's too garish," Devin stated loud enough for all to hear.

The clerk's expression faltered for a split second. "We have many other fine—"

"I think this is the one," said Lucas. He boldly reached out to touch the stones, brushing his fingertips against the warm, soft skin of Devin's chest. His voice went lower. "This is definitely the one."

"No," said Devin.

"Oh, yes," said Lucas. He hadn't thought about buying her jewelry. But suddenly he wanted Devin to look exactly like this at the party tonight. He wanted to watch her sinuous movements under the slinky dress, to see her smile, to hear her voice and to pretend it was a real date.

"You're going to meet the Duke of Rothcliff," he told her. "I'm expanding our manufacturing base in Europe, and I need to impress him."

"That's ridiculous."

"It's a time-honored tradition. I wear the same old tired suit, and you're the billboard for my wealth."

Devin's jaw worked for a moment.

"Now *that's* a ball gown," Byron said in a hearty voice from the chair next to them.

Lucas looked up, and Devin turned her head.

"Too much?" asked Lexi as she did a twirl in a fuchsia satin strapless dress with miles of ruffled, bell-shaped skirt.

"I'm finding us a big ol' ball to attend," Byron responded. "Hell, I'd even strap myself into a tux to take you out in that, darlin'."

Lexi's grin was wide.

"No, to the necklace," Devin told Lucas.

But Lucas had already reached in his pocket and deftly extracted a credit card. "Yes, to the necklace," he told the clerk. "Yes to the dress. And yes to everything else she's wearing."

His credit card was out of his hand before Devin could mount another protest, and the clerk was swiftly heading across the store.

"I win," he told Devin.

"What did you win?" she scoffed. "You just spent—" She faltered. "Lucas, you didn't ask the price."

"It'll be on the bill," he told her mildly.

"Are you showing off?" she challenged.

"Yeah. Because up until now, I didn't think you knew I had money."

"You're impossible."

"What was your first clue?"

She pointed in the direction the clerk had gone. "Go stop her."

"Yeah, right."

"Lucas."

He lifted his eyebrows.

"What are you doing?"

"We're shopping for dresses. Which, by the way, is a whole lot more fun than I expected."

Byron chuckled beside them. "Take that one, too," he called to Lexi. "And try on something else. Lucas is finally starting to have some fun here."

"You go try on something else," Lucas told Devin, enjoying the way her eyes flashed blue fire.

"And bankrupt the company?" she asked.

"We can afford it."

"Is this the way you're going to manage Amelia's money?"

"Amelia's too young for diamonds."

"You know what I mean."

"That was on my personal credit card, Devin. I don't spend corporate money on a date."

She smoothed the dress and then rubbed her bare arms. "Lucas, I am *really* uncomfortable about this."

"You afraid I'll expect you to put out?" he dared. He expected her to blush, or get flustered, or get angry.

Instead, she straightened, took a breath and looked him square in the eyes. "I already have."

As she turned to flounce away, Lucas found himself under Byron's accusing stare.

"What do you want from me?" Lucas asked him. "I bought the woman some diamonds."

Byron didn't pick up on the joke. "You don't think you might be playing a bit of a dangerous game here?"

Lucas turned to face the older man head on, acknowledging to himself, as well as to Byron, the magnitude of the stakes. "You think I haven't already thought of that?"

Devin had never thought of herself as particularly starstruck, but meeting a member of the royal family had put a cluster of butterflies firmly in her stomach. She found herself glad to be wearing a designer dress, and of the confidence boost from the diamond necklace.

"Do you do this kind of thing a lot?" she asked Lucas as they moved from the ballroom to the veranda of the Oak Point Country Club. The evening was sultry and warm. Little white lights decorated the railings and palm trees. The veranda overlooked a rolling lawn that sloped down to a narrow river. Pathways led across a footbridge to the lighted gardens beyond.

"Eat dinner or meet royalty?" Lucas stopped when the reached the rail.

"Hang out with the who's who." Even as she asked the question, she knew the answer. Lucas held an important position, in an important company. She might not be an economics expert, but she understood high tech was the future for well-paying jobs in the country. "Never mind," she added.

"You look very beautiful," he told her, eyes a soft pewter in subtle light.

"It's the hair."

"And the face."

"It took three highly skilled professionals to get me looking like this."

"That's not what I meant."

Uncomfortable, she turned to face the rail, bracing her hands and gazing out across the grounds of the country club. "Are you flirting with me?"

"Absolutely." He moved in behind her, his voice intimate behind her ear.

"Do you think that's such a good idea?"

"I think it's a terrible idea." He stroked the backs of his fingers down her bare arm. "If we flirt, I figure there's a better than even chance we'll end up in bed."

She started to call him on his bold assertion, but he kept right on talking.

"And, after we make love, there's a better than even chance we'll fight." He drew a breath. "And I don't like the way that pattern ends."

A gust of wind flitted through the palm trees, rustling the leaves above them. Partygoers made their way up and down the stairs to the lawn below, talking and laughing while strains of the string quartet wafted out from the dining room.

Lucas was right. If anything, the sexual pull between them was growing stronger. She was dressed up in diamonds and great shoes, and she was at a snazzy party with exciting guests, and she was standing out here on a sultry evening with the sexiest man she'd ever met. She wanted nothing more than to throw caution to the wind and flirt the night away.

But first, she owned him some honesty.

She turned. "I'm really sorry, Lucas."

He nodded, easing back a couple of inches. "Understood."

"I should never have looked at Konrad's emails," she continued. "I was wrong. And I knew it at the time. And, please believe me, I was about to stop." She closed her eyes for a brief second. "But, for a minute there, the end seemed to justify the means."

"Are you asking me to take your word on that?"

She opened her eyes again. "Yes. I am."

"Okay."

"You will?"

"Yes."

"Really?" Her heart lightened.

"I will. Now, will you take my word on something?"

She hesitated, bracing to see how he'd push his agenda. "What?"

"You are drop-dead gorgeous, and it has absolutely nothing to do with the dress, the diamonds or the shoes."

Awareness prickled her skin in the thick, moist air, and she reached to touch the necklace that had warmed against her skin.

"Though, I admit, I am partial to your new underwear."

"How do you know I'm wearing it?" she teased.

"No panty lines." He glanced down at her neckline. "And I can see the lace from the bra."

Devin sucked in a breath, as Lucas shifted closer, slipping

a hand to the small of her back, lowering it ever so slowly to the curve of her buttocks. The lacey underwear suddenly felt sinfully delicious. She inhaled the scent of his skin, reveled in the vibration of his deep voice and struggled not to move under his feathery touch.

"I never would have slept with you," she told him, "if I didn't want to do it."

"Glad to hear that." His head tipped to one side, and his lips parted.

"Not here," she whispered, cursing the fact they were in full view of the other guests.

"Afraid we'll shock the royalty?"

"Afraid you have more in mind than a kiss."

"I have *way* more in mind than a kiss."

"That will have to wait until we get home."

"Define home."

"The ranch."

Lucas's hand tightened on her rear end, snuggling her up against his body. "Uh-uh. No way." He jerked his head to one side. "See that big building over there? That's the Gulf Port Grand Hotel."

"We're not staying in Houston."

"Oh, yes we are. You don't get to tease me like that, then expect me to make it all the way back to Dallas."

"Tease you?"

"The underwear."

"You bought the underwear."

"You wore it."

"It matched the dress."

His gaze went to her neckline again. "You'll be lucky if I make it to the hotel."

"What about Lexi and Byron? It's his airplane."

"You don't think I could get my own airplane down here? And Byron already has a reservation at the hotel."

"He does not." Devin refused to believe Byron intended to seduce Lexi. Not that she thought Lexi would object. But it sounded as though they hadn't even kissed yet.

Lucas surreptitiously stroked the pad of his thumb along her collarbone. "He bought her three dresses and an emerald watch, you don't think he's hoping for a romantic ending to the night?"

Devin allowed herself a small shudder at the touch, but then she determinedly pushed his hand away. "You bought me a diamond necklace," she accused.

He grunted. "And I expect you to put out."

"Are you trying to pick a fight?"

"No. Absolutely not." He twined their fingers together. "Why? Are you getting mad?"

"No," she admitted. Then she reached out and straightened his silk charcoal tie and ran her palms down the front of his shirt. She curved her mouth into a sultry smile. "And, just so you know, I am going to put out."

"Oh, man," he breathed, his hand convulsing over hers. "Get me to the limo."

Ten

In the giant bathtub of the Gulf Port Grand Hotel suite, Lucas handed Devin a flute of chilled champagne. He couldn't remember ever having a bubble bath before, but he loved the feel of Devin naked in his arms. Her slick little body was cradled between his thighs, and she lay back against his chest so that he could rest his chin on her fragrant hair.

"What are we celebrating?" she asked as she accepted the glass. Candles flickered in every corner of the room, and her skin glowed under their radiance.

He touched his crystal glass to hers. "To changing our pattern," he proposed.

"We're definitely not fighting," she observed.

And Lucas was hoping to keep it that way. He took a sip of the bubbly liquid.

Devin did the same. "Who'd have thought we'd have Steve to thank."

Lucas coughed on the champagne bubbles. "Steve doesn't deserve thanks for anything."

Devin selected a fresh strawberry from the glass bowl at the edge of the tub and popped it into her mouth. "I've decided to picture him home, alone in his sterile penthouse, rubbing his miserly hands together, unaware that he's headed for a life of loneliness and despair."

"Nice picture." Lucas chuckled. "I like it."

"Unlike you and I," Devin continued, sliding her wet leg along the inside of his thigh, "who are making the most of our enforced partnership."

"Is that what we're doing?"

"What would you call it?"

"Let me see." He pretended to ponder. He wrapped his free arm around her waist, enjoying the heat of her skin and the way she fit to his body. He tipped his face against her hair and couldn't resist giving her a gentle kiss. "Bliss," he told her.

She bit into another strawberry. "Bliss for us. Despair for Steve."

"And justice for Amelia."

Devin leaned her head back. "I think Monica would approve."

"So would Konrad." Lucas watched the candlelight flicker against the butter-yellow walls. It reflected back from the frosted bay window and made patterns against the ceiling. "Thank you, Devin."

She twisted in his arms, splashing water against the side of the tub. "For?"

"For agreeing to write the letter. For taking a chance on me."

"Do you miss Konrad?" she asked, leaning her head against his shoulder where she could look up into his face.

"Very much." Lucas took a sip of the champagne. "You know, it sounds trite, but it really is lonely at the top. I've been surrounded my whole life with people who want something from me. I've never known who to trust. I never know who my friends are. But Konrad was always there. And now he's not."

Lucas stopped talking, not sure why he'd confided in Devin.

"I missed Monica when she got married," said Devin. "And some nasty, terrible little part of me was glad when she left Konrad to come home."

"You're not nasty, and you're not terrible," he felt compelled to point out. She was compassionate and protective, supportive and loving, and Amelia was lucky to have her in her life.

"Maybe," Devin answered. "Of course, I'd have supported her unconditionally if she'd decided to go back to him. But I've spent very little of my life without her. Until now."

Lucas's heart went out to Devin. "What happened to your parents?"

"My dad left years ago. With his secretary if I remember the fights correctly. I never did ask my mom what happened. And I haven't a clue where he is." She took a breath. "Mom died when I was twenty. Monica was nineteen. Amelia seems like a miracle."

"I agree," said Lucas, smiling when he thought of his adorable niece. "Did I tell you I changed her messy diaper yesterday?"

"No way."

"I did," he confirmed.

Devin nudged him with a playful elbow. "You have any proof?"

"Ask Teresa."

"Teresa works for you."

"You think she'd lie?"

"I think she'd say whatever you told her to say."

"You're accusing me of a grand conspiracy over a dirty diaper?"

"I'm saying I saw you turn green that time at my house."

"Well, I've hardened off since then."

Devin set down her champagne glass and dipped her hand below the water. "Speaking of hard."

Lucas sucked in a breath. "Are you kidding me?"

"I am not kidding you." She turned to straddle his lap. Her breasts bobbed out of the water…slick, soapy and tantalizing.

He quickly set down his own glass as his body responded to the view. His hands automatically cradled her buttocks, sliding her fully up the length of his thighs. She bent to kiss him, her mouth hot while the steam wafted from the water to fill the space around them.

He cradled her face, kissing her deeply.

Somewhere in the recesses of his mind he asked himself what the hell he thought he was doing. He needed to hold back, keep some space between them. But all he seemed to want to do was bring her closer, hold her closer, let her in on the secrets he'd held dear for a lifetime.

He drew back to look at her. Her blue eyes were midnight dark. Her cheeks were flushed and dewy, her wispy hair damp from the steam. He stroked his thumb across her swollen red lips. Then he kissed her, kissed her harder, wrapped his arms fully around her and eased his body into hers.

He breathed her name, his body arching, his heart contracting.

"Lucas," she whispered back. "Oh, Lucas."

She wrapped her lithe body around him, and he swore he was never going to let her go.

Devin knew she was being influenced by Lucas. But she couldn't seem to help herself. From her vantage point on the cushy deck furniture on Byron's wide front porch, she was watching him roll a big colored ball for Amelia across the expanse of emerald lawn, while Amelia squealed in delight and toddled after it.

"I know he seems brash and cocky when you talk to him," Lexi was saying. "But he's really very gentle and respectful."

Her laptop in front of her, Devin had been trying to compose her letter to the judge for a good half hour. But she kept getting distracted. Lexi was the latest distraction, plunking herself down on a chair across from Devin, a glass of diet cola in her hand, hair in a messy ponytail.

"Are you talking about last night?" Devin couldn't help but ask. Like Devin and Lucas, Lexi and Byron had spent the night at the Gulf Port Grand Hotel.

"Last night, yesterday, this morning." Lexi took a sip of her drink. "I don't know what to think."

Devin glanced around to make sure they were alone. "So, uh, did you two…"

If Lexi's bright eyes and flushed face at breakfast this morning hadn't confirmed what Devin suspected, her smile did now.

Lexi leaned forward. "I slept with Byron." She compressed her lips on what was obviously trying to be an enormous grin. "And I wasn't even nervous. I wasn't uncomfortable. I wasn't even embarrassed." She sat back again. "I tell you, Devin, if you'd asked me a month ago if we'd be having this conversation, I'd have laughed in your face."

"That's so great." Devin was thrilled for her friend.

"It is, isn't it?" She gazed off into space for a moment. "I have no idea where it goes from here. I mean, he's talking about coming back to Seattle for a while. But, you know, we really just met."

Devin nodded to Lexi's wrist. "Let me see that watch."

Lexi glanced down at the diamond face and the delicate gold-and-emerald band. "I don't think this is a big deal for him."

"I do," said Devin. "I think taking you to the party was a big deal. I think bringing you here was a big deal. Lucas says that Byron's barely dated since Lucas's mother died."

"He talked about her," said Lexi. "He misses her. Like I miss Rick."

"That's sweet," said Devin.

Lexi gestured to Lucas and Amelia with her glass. "Now *that's* sweet."

"That's surprising," said Devin. Though, even as she said the words, she acknowledged that it didn't seem at all strange now to see Lucas playing with Amelia. It had been a rocky start, but the two of them had obviously grown very fond of each other.

"So, how was your night?" Lexi gave a meaningful waggle of her brows.

"Are you kidding? We were in a luxury hotel suite. Champagne, strawberries, a tub the size of a backyard pool and a view of the city that stretched for fifty miles."

"That's not what I'm asking."

"It was strange," Devin admitted.

Lexi gathered herself up on the chair and leaned in closer, eyes alight. "Strange how?"

Devin tossed a pillow at her. "Not that kind of strange."

"I'm not judging."

"There's nothing to judge. We—" Devin stopped herself. Lexi didn't need to know they'd made love in the tub. "What was strange, was that it seemed so normal to be with Lucas."

It truly had.

Making love with Lucas, talking with Lucas, sleeping in his arms, even waking up to shower and join Lexi and Byron for breakfast had, for some reason, seemed completely normal. Which didn't make sense. Since they were still most definitely at odds over Amelia's future.

She glanced down at the half-composed letter on her laptop. Well, they *would* still be at odds. But later, once they'd put Steve in his place.

"What are you writing?" asked Lexi.

"It's a letter to the judge. I'm trying to get the words just right. Obviously, I want to undermine Steve. But I don't want to set Lucas up for later." She drummed her fingertips on the arms of the chair.

Lexi glanced to where the two were playing on the lawn. "You don't think he'll still go after Amelia."

"Oh, I know he'll still go after Amelia. He thinks it's the right thing to do." And in a strange way, Devin had to admire that. "He thinks he's the only one who can protect her in the long term. He says Steve isn't the only threat. If I'm guardian, the jackals will constantly be circling."

"Even if he did win guardianship, do you really think he would take her away from you?"

"Are you arguing Lucas's side?"

"I'm just saying." Lexi swirled the ice cubes in her drink. "He's not as bad as I expected. And I think he likes you. And you might just be able to trust him."

Devin glared at Lexi for a long moment. Then she moved her attention to Lucas, who caught her gaze and gave her a wave, his familiar expression open and direct. Then he said something to Amelia and motioned for her to wave. She did. And Devin's heart squeezed tight.

Did she dare put her trust in Lucas?

* * *

"That kind of betrayal ought to be criminal." Byron smacked down the copy of the Seattle newspaper that had arrived at the ranch by courier.

"No argument from me," said Lucas from his armchair in front of Byron's stone fireplace, tumbler of single malt in his hand.

Steve had given an interview and laid out a series of false accusations about Konrad, naming Lucas as an accomplice and painting Monica as a naive victim and Amelia as a usurper. There was a picture with the article of Steve and his lovely new fiancée. They were at a charity event, handing over a big check.

Lucas was going to have to head back to Seattle soon, if only to salvage his reputation.

"You have to move fast on this," said Byron.

Lucas agreed. "Devin is writing me a letter for the judge."

"That's a coup."

"Tell me about it." Lucas took a sip of the Scotch.

"What did she say?"

Lucas shrugged. "She was working on it today. I'm not expecting miracles."

"Not even after last night?"

Lucas gave Byron a "back off" glare. He wasn't discussing his personal relationship with Devin. Though, last night had been nothing short of spectacular.

But it wasn't the lovemaking.

When he thought back, what he remembered was her sense of humor, the emotion in her eyes when she talked about Monica and her mother, the joy she obviously got from raising Amelia. And he remembered feeling jealous. It was the strangest sensation. He wanted to be part of Devin's inner circle, and simply making love to her wasn't enough to get him there.

"You know how I felt about your mother." Byron's voice had gone contemplative, and Lucas looked up.

"I know," Lucas acknowledged.

"We had our ups and downs. An uncouth cowboy from

Texas daring to court one of the richest women in the Pacific Northwest. A woman ten years older than him."

"You're not uncouth."

"I'm not urbane."

That was true enough.

"My point is," Byron continued, "we both knew it was worth it. All the heartache and pain, the snide remarks, the criticism… though, trust me—" he gestured with his tumbler "—I'd have protected her from it if I could."

"I know you would have."

"But it doesn't come along very often."

What was Byron saying? Did he think Lucas should grab hold of Devin? Maybe never let her go?

Lucas turned the idea over in his mind.

"A love like that," Byron mused, gazing at the amber liquid while he turned his glass against the lamplight. "You don't want to let it go."

Love?

Lucas stilled.

Did Byron think Lucas had fallen in love with Devin?

Was Lucas in love with Devin?

How would he know? How could he tell?

"I don't know for sure with Lexi," said Byron.

Lucas gave his head a little shake at the unexpected turn of the conversation.

"But I know the signs." Byron downed the remainder of his drink. "And I'm following her back to Seattle. And I'm pursuing her until she tells me to stop."

"Lexi?" asked Lucas. "But, you've only just—"

"Met her?" Byron asked. "Like I said, Lucas. I've been through this before. It's rare as hens' teeth. So is Lexi. I can't believe somebody hasn't snapped her up already."

"You're serious."

"You bet your boots I'm serious. I'm a serious man. Now. Back to Steve. He's really starting to worry me."

"He's worrying me, too," Lucas admitted. He'd gone over

worst-case scenarios in his mind, and any one of them could conceivably come true.

A judge might disinherit Amelia. Steve might get married and have a baby. The balance of power could potentially shift to him. And then Lucas would have to do something drastic, like sell his shares in Pacific Robotics and start over again.

When he thought about starting over again, he pictured Devin and Amelia as a permanent part of in his life. He stretched the image out in his mind. Amelia at five, ten, in high school and driving a car. She was going to be drop-dead beautiful. He knew that already.

Would Devin consider letting him stick around? Would she consider pursuing their relationship, maybe making it permanent? Did she feel anywhere close to how he was feeling?

He polished off his drink.

"I've had the boys sniff around a little bit more," Byron added. "They've got the name of the judge, and they threw together a little history of her decisions. It ain't good, Lucas. It ain't good a'tall."

"Devin's writing the letter," said Lucas.

"Better be one hell of a letter."

Lucas doubted that. "And I have a backup plan," he declared. He'd just come up with it. Right this very second. But, as Byron had said, when it was right, it was right.

"Do tell," Byron prompted.

"Devin. Me. Babies."

Byron slapped his knee and cackled. "You think you'll convince that pretty little gal to have your babies?"

Lucas struggled not to be insulted. Sure, maybe he didn't deserve Devin, but he wasn't the worst catch in the world. "I'm not saying I won't have to work at it."

"And just how fast d'you think you can accomplish that feat?" Byron tapped his blunt finger against the newspaper. "Steve's out there in public posing with his fiancée."

Lucas leaned forward, making certain he was clear and concise. "If I have to, I can work very fast. Hell, Konrad did."

And if Lucas didn't have to work fast, he'd work slow. He'd be patient, romantic and thorough in order to win Devin's love.

Ironically, Lucas felt better than he had in weeks, months, maybe years. Let Steve try his best. Lucas would fight back with everything he had. And, one way or another, he'd win. Because the goalposts had just shifted for him. He'd give up Pacific Robotics entirely for Devin and Amelia.

"But it's only the backup plan," he told Byron. "We'll see what she writes in the letter."

At the bottom of the ranch-house staircase, as Lucas's damning words washed over her, Devin held the signed letter between her hands and methodically tore it in half. Then she tore it again and again. She struggled for breath, shock and anger pulsing through her while she turned away. The staircase was long, her steps leaden as she headed back up to Amelia's room.

She might be under a court order to stay with Lucas, but surely any judge in the world would understand why she had to leave him.

She paused outside Amelia's room, gripping the doorjamb to hold herself steady, trying to put her thoughts into some kind or order. Lucas was using her. Getting her pregnant was his backup plan? He'd seduced her, made love with her, made her care about him, just in case Amelia was disinherited and he needed another baby?

How could she have been so colossally stupid? She should have seen it coming from miles away. What were the odds that he'd fallen for her? Exactly zero. He needed Amelia. And, if that didn't work, well any old baby would do. Any old woman would do, too.

He must have worked awfully hard to hold down his gag reflex with Amelia's smelly diapers and general stickiness. Devin cringed. He'd probably had to hold down his gag reflex with her, too. Lexi was right that the rich were nasty. And Lucas Demarco was an amoral monster.

She should call him on it. Right here, right now. She should force him to own up to exactly what he'd been up to these past weeks. Her feet nearly started moving, before she realized the danger. He'd never admit it. He'd lie his way out of it, just like he always did, and she would have blown her only chance to get away. She couldn't fight with Lucas. She had to escape from Lucas.

She had to pack up Amelia, get away from him and hide until a date could be set for the guardianship hearing.

Then she'd throw herself on the mercy of the judge.

She would tell the truth, the whole truth. She'd demonstrate exactly how Lucas and Konrad had behaved.

"Devin?"

Devin jumped at the sound of Lexi's voice and the gentle hand on her shoulder.

"You okay?" asked Lexi.

Devin shook her head, hot tears forming at the backs of her eyes.

Lexi turned her around. "Honey? What's wrong. You're white as a ghost."

"It's…" Devin was going to cry.

She couldn't let herself cry over that horrible man. She swallowed. "Lucas just told Byron I was his backup plan."

Lexi looked confused. "Backup for what?"

Devin opened the door and pulled Lexi into the bedroom, dropping her voice to a whisper. "I'm leaving. Right away. Right now. You have to help me get away."

Lexi looked stunned. "What are you talking about? I don't understand."

"It was a plot. Just like Konrad. From the very beginning, it's all been about the money." Devin clenched her fists and tipped her head back. "How, oh, how did I fall for it?"

"Honey, what happened?"

Devin let out a slightly hysterical laugh, and then quickly covered her mouth with her fingers. "Lucas just told Byron that if Amelia was disinherited, me having his baby was his backup plan. He said he might have to work at it, but he could work fast."

Lexi staggered back. "He said this to Byron?"

Devin nodded. "Byron asked how fast he thought he could do it."

Now Lexi had blanched. "So, Byron's in on it?"

"They are a conspiratorial lot, those Demarcos."

Lexi's jaw clamped down, and she grasped Devin's arm. "Are you positive?"

"I am positive."

"Then we have to get you out of here."

"I know."

"You get Amelia," Lexi instructed. "There are pickup trucks in the yard with the keys inside."

"We're stealing a truck?"

"We'll leave a message. They can come and pick it up from the airport. Go."

"Right," Devin agreed. But then she stumbled.

What would they do? Where would they go? And if Devin hid Amelia against the judge's order, was she kidnapping her?

Could Lucas use it against her?

She realized he could. And she realized he would. And she couldn't risk compromising her case.

An overwhelming sense of helplessness engulfed her. "The judge said I had stay at the Demarco mansion."

Lexi's hands went to her hips. "Well, that's not going to work."

"I can't kidnap her. It would completely compromise my case."

They both blinked at each other. There was no solution. There was absolutely no solution.

"What if we could get them to hold the hearing right away?" Lexi asked.

"I don't think it's like a hair appointment." Devin doubted they could call up and see if there'd been a cancellation.

Lexi clicked her tongue for a few moments. Then she snapped her fingers.

"What?" Devin didn't dare hope.

"There's one other person on this planet who wants the hearing to happen fast."

Devin didn't follow.

"And I'll just bet he's got the contacts and the clout to do it," Lexi explained.

As the truth set in, Devin felt her stomach congeal to wet cement. "Steve."

Lexi gave a slow, deliberate nod. And Devin knew it was their only choice.

The next night, in the mansion's great room, Lucas could barely contain his frustration with Devin as he faced three members of the Pacific Robotics Board of Directors. All three were loyal to him, and all three were obviously both angry and worried.

"I thought you said you had it under control," Craig Grenville opened, a hard edge to his voice. His snifter of brandy sat untouched on the table beside him.

"I *did* have it under control." Lucas had been blindsided by Devin's disappearance.

"But, she's gone," Peter Huntley stated in a flat tone. He'd drained his brandy glass and was glancing around for more.

"I can't even begin to guess why she took off." At first, Lucas had thought they'd been kidnapped.

But when it seemed certain she'd left of her own free will, he started searching for reasons. "There was no evidence that Steve made contact with her," he confirmed for the Board members. "And none of the reporters found us in Texas."

"We need a plan B," Ivan Rusk spoke up. He pushed his glasses up on the bridge of his nose, crossing and uncrossing his lanky legs as he spoke. "If Steve gets control, you *know* we're all fired the next day."

Lucas scoffed, "What plan B, where plan B?" His lawyers had already contacted him with an early court date for the guardianship trial. It had been reset for next week at Devin's lawyer's insistence. So it was obviously going to happen before Steve's petition to appeal the will.

Lucas couldn't begin to guess what Devin would say on the

stand. Or maybe he could. The fact that she'd snuck away from Byron's ranch in the middle of the night told him a lot. Nothing she said in the guardianship hearing would help either Lucas or Amelia's case when it came time to hear the appeal of the will.

What the *hell* was she thinking?

Byron set the bottle of brandy down on the bar and pivoted to face the men. "Well, I've got myself a plan B."

They waited while he took a step closer to the grouping of couches and overstuffed armchairs.

He drew a deep breath. "We get Bob, my ranch vet, to geld Steve."

There was a moment of stunned silence, before Peter burst out laughing.

Both Ivan and Craig stared at him as if he'd lost his mind.

"And then," Peter sputtered. "Lucas can take his sweet time having as many children as he wants. I like it."

Craig frowned in disgust. "If amateur hour is over at The Improv, can we get back to the problem at hand?"

Lucas hid his smile behind a swallow of brandy. He knew Byron's suggestion was ridiculous, but that didn't mean he couldn't like it. Lucas realized he'd want to have those children with Devin, which was obviously impossible. He had to forcibly tamp down a wave of despair.

"What's she going to say in court?" Ivan asked him point blank.

Lucas admitted to himself that Devin was a wild card, never more so than now. "She knows the stakes for Amelia," he answered evasively.

"Could she have found something out?" asked Ivan.

"Yeah," Craig added. "Like the truth about her sister's marriage?"

"There's no truth for her to find out," Lucas all but shouted. "Konrad *loved* Monica."

"You're protesting a little too much," said Craig.

Lucas pinned him with an angry glare. "I'm protesting exactly the correct amount. Konrad's not here to defend himself—"

"Understand our positions," said Ivan. Sweat had popped out on his forehead. "Steve knows we've been loyal to you."

Byron moved ever so subtly to position himself behind Lucas. "I'd hoped y'all were loyal to honor and integrity. And that was something you had in common with Lucas."

Peter lifted his glass in a toast to Lucas. "If Steve takes over, I'm walkin'."

Lucas gave Peter a nod of appreciation, admiring the man's reliability.

Craig sat forward. "It's not that simple."

"It's exactly that simple," said Peter, all traces of humor gone. "Either you're with us or against us."

"Code of the West," said Byron.

"This isn't some classic movie. Good guys against the bad guys," said Craig. "It's complicated. And we have to think strategically. There might still be time to come to a deal with Steve."

"Nobody's making any deal," Lucas stated with conviction.

"Speak for yourself." Craig came to his feet. And after a moment's hesitation, Ivan came to his also.

Lucas slowly rose to face them. "You two have obviously made your choice."

"The writing's on the wall," said Craig. "Steve's star witness is going to support him."

Ivan tugged at his collar.

"Then good luck to you, boys," Byron offered in a falsely hearty tone. "I hope Steve welcomes you both with open arms."

There was a minute of uncomfortable silence before the two men left.

As the door banged shut, Peter leaned back and stretched his legs out on the rug in front of him. "Well, good to have the rats off the ship, I guess."

Lucas grunted. "The ship's still sinking."

Peter swirled the golden brandy in the bottom of his glass and gave a shrug. "I can swim."

Byron ambled over to an armchair and eased down into the thick cushions. "At least those two won't be in the water to steal our life preservers."

Lucas couldn't help but chuckle. "I don't think we have life preservers. I think Devin is going to hold our heads under until we stop struggling."

"You must have really ticked her off," Byron ventured.

Lucas wished he knew what he'd done. If he had a clue, he could at least try to fight back.

The ocean waves bubbled up on the rocky beach of the secluded San Juan Islands resort where Devin was holed-up with Amelia and Lexi.

Her lawyer Hannah Snow had taken the ferry from Seattle and now joined them on the wooden deck in front of the cottage, shaded by massive cedar trees that blocked the hot, noonday sun.

"Your only job is to tell the truth," said Hannah, crossing her tanned legs beneath a simple, sleeveless, white linen dress. "The decision is up to the judge."

Devin hated the thought of playing into Steve's hand. But she wouldn't lie to protect Lucas. She could live with any outcome, except for one where she lost Amelia.

"The judge understands why I left?"

Hannah nodded. "I only get to tell the truth, too. But I gave the judge a written brief. She'll know you didn't maliciously kidnap Amelia."

Devin's stomach clamped tight. "You didn't use the word *kidnap.*"

Hannah reached out to pat Devin's knee. "Certainly not. I told her about the reporters, and that you had to leave the mansion on short notice."

Lexi chimed in from the padded, wooden bench swing where she'd curled up in a corner. "And that's not shading the truth."

Hannah quirked a smile. "No, it's not. I also told her about Texas."

Devin leaned her head back, scrunching her eyes shut against the crackling, blue sky. "I just want this to be over."

Hannah came to her feet. "It'll be over in three more days. You'll come to the office Thursday morning?"

"I will," Devin agreed. "Lexi is going to stay with Amelia."

"Good. We'll go over your testimony then."

"Am I allowed to give my opinion on the stand?" Devin couldn't help remembering Lucas's accusations about hearsay and opinion versus fact.

"The truth as you remember it," said Hannah, straightening her purse over her shoulder. "That's all you need to do."

"And let the chips fall where they may," Devin couldn't help muttering.

"The judge will make sure it's fair, reasonable and legal."

"Why doesn't that make me feel any better?"

Hannah's expression was compassionate. "You know worrying won't help, right?"

Devin nodded. She was trying hard not to worry, but so many things were going wrong in her life lately.

"Thursday, then?"

"I'll be there."

Hannah took her leave down the short staircase to the resort road where her rental car waited.

"I hope I'm not making a huge mistake," Devin said, as the engine caught and Hannah put the sedan into reverse.

"Have you fully considered your other options?"

Devin had done nothing but fully consider her other options for three nights running. But there were no other viable alternatives. She couldn't trust Lucas. She couldn't trust Steve. And she couldn't commit perjury for anyone.

"There are boats to Canada every day of the week," Lexi pointed out. "Just say the word."

Devin appreciated the sentiment, and the unwavering support, but going on the run was yet another non-viable option.

"I have to believe I won't lose custody," she stated. It was the only thing keeping her sane.

"I absolutely believe you'll win custody," said Lexi with a

decisive nod. "Lucas is going to look like the manipulative creep that he is, and, in the end, you're going to chalk this all up to experience."

Devin forced out a laugh. "What doesn't kill me, makes me stronger?"

"What doesn't kill you, is fodder for your next book."

"There is that," Devin agreed.

She'd spoken to her editor last week, and they were interested in her book idea for *Nice and Rich*. They were also willing to give her an extension on the deadline for *Snarled Traffic in the Information Age*. Thank goodness.

"I'll have to find a new rich family to study," Devin pointed out.

"Byron might—" Lexi snapped her mouth shut.

A chill washed over Devin. "Are you still planning to see Byron?"

Lexi vigorously shook her head. "No. I don't know what I was thinking. That just kind of slipped out."

"Do you want to see Byron?" Devin was embarrassed to admit that her friend's happiness hadn't even crossed her mind. But it did now, and she felt incredibly selfish. Lexi and Byron had really seemed to have something going.

"No way," Lexi denied. "How would I ever trust him? He was in on it the whole time. You caught Lucas talking openly to him about their schemes. No, I'm not going to see him. I don't want to."

Devin took in the flush on Lexi's face, and the way she plucked at her khaki shorts while she talked, her gaze darting from her shorts, to her toes, and back again.

An unsettling thought came over Devin. "Lexi? Did you fall in love with Byron?"

Lexi blinked to meet Devin's gaze straight on. "Did you fall in love with Lucas?"

Devin's heart thumped deep in her chest, while pain tightened the cavity around it. Her throat closed up, and when she finally spoke, there was a catch to her voice. "I don't know."

Eleven

Three days later, Devin climbed from a taxi into the bright sunshine in front of the Seattle courthouse. She straightened her blazer and smoothed the matching skirt. Then she ran light fingertips over her hair to make sure everything was in place. She wanted to look every inch the credible witness and capable mother-figure for this.

Before she could move, Lucas appeared in front of her on the sidewalk, grasping her by the arm and pulling her over to one side. "Are you *out of your mind?*" he demanded.

She'd braced herself for seeing him today, made sure her anger was fresh and her defenses were firmly in place. But the minute he was there in front of her, memories pushed at the wall she'd built up, and her chest contracted with emotion.

"What the hell happened to you?" he growled. "One minute we were together, and the next you'd disappeared into the night."

"Together?" she reflexively choked out, commanding her legs to start moving. She'd promised herself she wouldn't talk to him directly. Everything this smooth-talking, persuasive man had to say, could be said in front of the judge.

She fought his grip as she marched toward the steps.

He kept pace beside her, and she glanced around for her lawyers. Steve had said they'd meet her here.

"I *trusted* you," Lucas persisted.

Devin clamped her jaw, refusing the temptation to engage in a debate.

"You're handing it to him. You have to know that. You're betraying me, and you're betraying Amelia."

"Betraying?" Her low voice shook with repressed fury.

"Yes. We could have worked this—"

"*You* betrayed *me*. I was your *backup plan,* Lucas. You're as bad as Konrad. You're worse than Konrad."

Lucas's hand dropped from her arm, and it took her a second to realize he'd stopped dead in his tracks.

Good. She hadn't wanted to talk to him anyway. She increased her pace. She was only steps from the door. Once she was inside, she'd be home free—nothing to do but testify and win permanent guardianship of Amelia. Nothing.

But he caught up again, tone incredulous. "*What* did you say?"

She ignored him.

"*Devin.*"

She gave in to temptation. "You heard me. Well, really, I heard you talking to Byron. 'Devin. Me. Babies.' I believe that's an exact quote."

Lucas was silent for a full, stunned second. "You misunderstood."

She whirled to face him, jamming her thumb against her chest. "I misunderstood. Monica misunderstood. How many other people misunderstand your despicable conspiracies?"

"My backup plan," he enunciated, voice scoffing as he leaned in, "was falling in love with you."

She ignored the constriction of her chest. "Oh, you're good."

The man would say anything if he thought it would put her off balance.

"I was telling Byron that if worse came to worst, and we lost Pacific Robotics, I was grateful that I'd still have you." Lucas's expression was open and frank, and for a second there, she almost fell for it.

But then she mentally smacked herself, turned on her heel and marched into the courthouse.

Inside, she was swallowed up by Steve's team of lawyers, who escorted her to the front of the courtroom. She barely heard their last-minute instructions, and though she caught movement in her peripheral vision, so she knew Lucas's team had sat down, she kept her gaze fixed firmly ahead.

The judge began to speak, but Devin was fighting a ringing in her ears. Her palms were sweating, and her mouth had gone dry. Lucas was lying. He was absolutely lying about falling in love with her.

She needed to concentrate on Amelia. Amelia was back at the San Juan Islands resort with Lexi where they'd spent the last few days. Devin and Lexi had joked about taking a boat to Canada and hiding Amelia until she turned eighteen. Right now, it didn't seem like such a bad idea.

"Ms. Hartley?" the judge prompted, and the lawyer next to Devin nudged her.

"Yes, Your Honor?"

"Please take the witness stand."

Devin rose shakily to her feet, surreptitiously smoothing her damp palms down the side of her charcoal-gray skirt. She walked carefully on her high heels, keeping her gaze fixed on points along the walls—the flag, a water pitcher, an antique portrait, the judge's gavel.

She climbed into the witness stand and swore to tell the truth. She couldn't wait to tell the truth.

Her lawyer went first, and the opening questions were innocuous, factual. They'd rehearsed them a dozen times. She talked about Monica and Konrad's whirlwind courtship, the fact that she was surprised at how quickly Monica became pregnant, and that Monica hadn't known about the inheritance until she'd overheard Lucas and Konrad discussing her pregnancy.

Partway through her testimony, Steve slipped into the courtroom and took a seat at the back of the gallery. There were few other spectators, except for the overflow of lawyers sitting in the gallery benches directly behind each of the tables.

Devin's lawyer gave her an encouraging nod and a wink, then he sat back down at the table.

One of Lucas's lawyers stood up. "Did your sister love Konrad Demarco?" he asked without preamble, dropping his pencil and moving from behind the table and into the center of the courtroom.

Devin leaned slightly into the microphone. "I believe she did."

"What makes you believe she loved him?"

Devin couldn't help a reflexive glance in Lucas's direction, reminded of their conversations about what she knew for certain and what she only surmised. "She told me that she loved him."

"Was she excited to get married?"

"Yes."

"Was she excited to be pregnant?"

Devin nodded. "Yes."

"Did your sister believe Konrad loved her?"

Devin hesitated, trying to remember what Monica had specifically said about Konrad's love for her.

She remembered the wedding photos. She pictured their early months together, Monica with her arms wrapped around Konrad's neck, his whispered words to her, her grin, the way his hand encircled her waist, the way his eyes lit up when he spoke her name, and the way he watched her from across the room, like nobody else on earth existed.

"Ms. Hartley?"

"I'm sorry." She blinked to bring the lawyer back into focus. "What was the question?"

"Did your sister believe Konrad loved her?"

"Yes."

"Would you say they were happy together?"

"At first," Devin admitted.

"What changed?"

Devin's glanced drifted to Lucas again. "She found out it was all a scam. Lucas and Konrad wanted Amelia to inherit their grandfather's estate."

The lawyer moved closer, his voice going lower, less theatrical. "How did she find this out?"

"She overheard a conversation between Konrad and his brother Lucas."

"What did they say?"

"That they'd thwart Steve by having Amelia."

"Any chance your sister misunderstood their meaning?"

"No."

"Any chance she heard the words out of context?"

"No."

"How can you be so certain?"

"I spent the next year helping her get over Konrad's betrayal."

The lawyer backed off, and Devin took a breath. She tried hard not to meet Lucas's eyes, but she found her attention drawn in his direction, more and more frequently.

"And what did Konrad do during that year?" asked the lawyer.

"He tried to win her back." Devin said the words more to Lucas than to anyone else. "He tried every trick in the book to get her and Amelia to come back to him. But she wouldn't do it."

Lucas's lips compressed in a thin line.

"You believe Konrad was insincere?" asked the lawyer.

"Yes."

The lawyer looked to Lucas, and Lucas gave an almost imperceptible shake of his head.

The lawyer cocked his head sideways and waited.

Lucas shook again.

There was some kind of silent argument going on between them.

Then the lawyer turned back to Devin. "Ms. Hartley, I understand you broke into Lucas Demarco's personal email account."

Lucas brought his hand down on the table and started to rise, but another lawyer grasped his shoulder to hold him down.

"Ms. Hartley?"

"I didn't 'break' into it." There'd been no password. It was conceivable that she'd accidentally opened it.

"But you did look at Mr. Demarco's private emails."

Devin swallowed. "Yes."

"Why?"

Her voice came out slightly high-pitched, but the man was beginning to frustrate her. "To prove I was right."

"And did you prove that?"

Devin resettled herself in the witness chair and told herself to calm down. "I read an email from Lucas to Konrad that said, 'I'm counting on you.' They were talking about Monica."

"And you interpreted that to mean Lucas was counting on Konrad to woo Monica, marry her quickly and have a baby in order to capitalize on their grandfather's will."

"Yes."

"Is that what the email said?"

Devin didn't understand the question, and she gave her head a reflexive little shake.

"Was the email that specific?" asked the lawyer. "Did it go in to the details of the alleged plot, or did it simply say 'I'm counting on you'?"

"'I'm counting on you,'" Devin repeated.

"So, for all you know, Lucas could have been counting on Konrad to pick up a quart of milk on the way home?"

Devin's lawyer jumped to his feet. "Objection, Your Honor."

"I'll allow it," said the judge.

The lawyer carried on. "They could have been referring to anything."

"Maybe," Devin was forced to admit. "But—"

"Why would he try to win her back?" the lawyer shot out, startling Devin.

"Excuse me?"

"Why would Konrad, having already married Monica, already impregnated Monica, clearly having fulfilled the terms of his grandfather's will. Why would he then spend pretty much every waking minute for the next year trying to win her back?"

Devin hesitated.

Once again, she found her glance going to Lucas.

For some reason, he'd stopped looking aggressive. He almost looked compassionate. Was he feeling sorry for her? Was she doing so badly on the stand that she evoked his pity?

"He wanted her back because he loved her," said the lawyer.

"Speculation," said Devin's lawyer.

"Rephrase," said the judge.

The lawyer moved closer to Devin, speaking slowly and deliberately. "If Konrad had truly loved Monica, and if she had misunderstood a conversation between him and his brother, and if she had left him, what would you expect him to do?"

Devin paused. She knew she'd walked right into a trap. But there she was. She couldn't get out.

And the lawyer was right. If she took a giant step back from her sister's emotional upset, Konrad had done everything a man in love might do. Devin couldn't be positive he hadn't loved Monica. Nor could she be positive he'd manipulated her.

The truth came to Devin in a blinding wave.

Lucas was right. He'd been right all along, and she couldn't lie about it.

She looked directly at Lucas. "I'd expect a man in love to try to win his wife back."

Lucas gave Devin a ghost of a soft, compassionate smile. He looked genuinely regretful at the turns of events. He couldn't be, of course. By rights, he should be celebrating.

There was a strangled exclamation from the back of the room, as Steve threw up his hands in disgust.

"I ask again," said the lawyer to Devin, "is there any chance Monica misunderstood Konrad and Lucas's conversation?"

"Yes," Devin admitted, blinking against the sting of tears. Lucas was going to win it all. And he was going to take Amelia away from her. And she'd have to beg him for every second she spent with her niece.

The lawyer looked to Lucas again, and this time Lucas nodded.

"Why did you take Amelia away from the Demarco security last weekend?" asked the lawyer.

Here it was. The final nail in Devin's coffin. She drew a bracing breath. "I found out Lucas was manipulating me." She stopped talking, feeling sick to her stomach. Was Lucas really going to make her admit in open court that they'd had an affair.

"Because you overheard a conversation?" asked the lawyer.

Devin nodded. Her throat was closing over and her stomach was in knots.

"Any chance you misunderstood?"

Devin started to shake her head.

But then she stopped, Lucas's earlier words ringing in her ears. *You misunderstood. My backup plan was falling in love with you.*

Her horrified gaze flew to him, and he cocked his head, raising his brows as if he was waiting for her to get the punch line.

Could it be? Was it possible?

"Ms. Hartley," the lawyer continued, "remembering that you are under oath. Are you in love with Lucas Demarco?"

"*Your Honor,*" objected Devin's lawyer.

"I don't see the relevance," the judge stated, in a warning tone.

"I promise you, it's relevant," said Lucas's lawyer.

The judge hesitated, while Devin's heart thudded deep in her chest. What should she do? What could she say? She didn't want to lie under oath, but how she felt about Lucas was none of these people's business.

While they all waited, Lucas stood and handed a folded note to his lawyer. The man read it and smiled.

The judge held out her hand, and the lawyer dutifully gave her the note.

Then the judge smiled and nodded, handing it back.

Devin braced herself for the question.

"Ms. Hartley, are you—"

"Yes!" she shouted. "Okay? Are you satisfied?" She glared at the judge. What kind of a thing was this to do to a woman?

Lucas's lawyer handed her the note.

Face hot with mortification, and refusing to meet anyone else's eyes, she opened up the stupid note. It read:

Full custody to Devin Hartley. Right here. Right now. If she loves me back. And if she'll agree to marry me.

Devin blinked and read it again, confusion warring with anger, warring with shock.

"One more question, Your Honor?" said the lawyer.

"By all means," said the judge, her tone tinged with mock capitulation as she rocked back in her high chair.

"Devin," said the lawyer, "is that a yes?"

Devin glanced up to see two dozen pairs of eyes on her. She looked to Lucas, and the enormity of the situation began to hit her. He loved her. He *loved* her?

Everything he'd said. Everything he'd done. Their days and nights together, and his affection for Amelia, it was all true?

"Five-minute recess," said the judge, bringing down her gavel.

Lucas was out of his seat in a shot, rushing to Devin, handing her down from the witness stand and pulling her into his arms.

"I love you," he told her, his words clear and heartfelt. "And I love Amelia. And I want you to marry me." Then he spoke over Devin's shoulder. "Your honor, can we dismiss the case or something?"

The judge met Devin's gaze and lifted her brows in a question. Devin couldn't help smiling with joy.

"I'm off at three," the judge quipped, her interest unabashed. "You know, in case you need someone to officiate."

Devin grinned, while Lucas laughed.

Steve stomped out of the courtroom.

"Three o'clock is good for me," said Devin, wrapping her

arms around Lucas and leaning into his embrace. "As long as we can get Lexi and Amelia here in time."

She drew a deep sigh, picturing the glorious years stretching out in front of them. "I love you so much," she confessed, absorbing Lucas's warmth and strength.

His lips came down on hers in a thorough kiss. "I'm going to love you forever."

The judge's gavel came down one more time. "Bailiff, call the florist. And somebody find these people a ring."

Devin twisted the simple silver ring around the finger of her left hand while she waited for Lucas to finish reading the galleys for *Snarled Traffic in the Information Age*. He'd bought her a diamond wedding set a few days after their rushed wedding, but she preferred the original, even if it had been purchased for twenty dollars at a souvenir shop across the street from the courthouse.

The maple leaves outside on the lighted grounds of the mansion flickered red and golden, and a small, gas fire danced in the depths of the stone fireplace in the great room. Amelia had celebrated her first birthday the week before. She was walking now, pulling articles off lower shelves and forcing the mansion staff to rearrange the art objects and antiques.

Lucas flipped the last page of the printed galleys.

"Well?" Devin asked, sitting up straight in the big armchair, feeling unaccountably anxious about his reaction.

He looked up at her and gave a mischievous grin.

"Don't you dare make me wait," she admonished.

Lucas came to his feet, crossing the room toward her. "I'd take your advice," he offered obliquely.

"Yeah?" She tipped her head as he came closer, deciding he meant it as a compliment.

"Especially the part about slowing down to enjoy the people you love." He took her hands in his and drew her to her feet, a gleam in his slate-gray eyes. "I'm going to enjoy loving you right here and now."

"That's not what I meant," she told him, with a playful smack to his upper arm. Still, she couldn't help the flutter of her heart as he leaned in for a kiss.

"Really?" His arms snaked around her, tugging her close. "You give the best advice I've ever read. And your book clearly stated that I ought to make love a priority in my life."

She sighed, relaxing into his strength, thinking back to last night, and the night before that, and the one before that. "I believe you already have."

"Well, we're still, technically, on our honeymoon."

"We've been married for over three months."

"I read somewhere that the honeymoon lasts for at least five years."

"Not in my book, you didn't."

"Then, you should add that part." He kissed her again, deeper this time, and his hand slipped beneath her blouse, sliding its way up her back.

Amelia was already asleep, but there were still a few staff members wandering around the house.

"Lucas," Devin warned.

"Hmm?"

"Get your hands away from my buttons."

He chuckled deep in his chest as the doorbell chimed in the front hallway.

Footsteps sounded in the hallway as one of the staff went to answer, and Lucas slowly drew back. He gave Devin a peck on the tip of her nose, whispering, "later."

Devin was fine with that.

Muffled voices sounded in the distance, and Devin quickly recognized Lexi's.

"They're back?" she asked Lucas. "Why didn't you say something?"

"I didn't know."

Just then, Byron's large frame filled the opening between the hallway and the great room, with Lexi clinging to his arm.

Devin squealed and rushed toward her friend. "How was the honeymoon? Did you like Tahiti?"

Lexi showed off a bare arm. "Take a look at my tan?"

Devin pulled her into a hug. "You look fabulous, healthy, rested."

The two men shook hands, and Lexi coughed out a laugh. "Not so much on the rested."

"She slept on the plane," said Byron, turning to wrap Devin in a warm hug, while Lucas did the same with Lexi.

"First chance I've had to sleep in two weeks," Lexi chided.

"She exaggerates," said Byron.

Devin drew back. "So, what did you decide? How long can you stay in Seattle?"

With Lexi's house here and Byron's ranch near Dallas, there was a pretty big geographical divide to overcome.

Byron and Lexi exchanged a look.

"What?" Devin prompted, hoping Lexi wouldn't have to leave immediately for Texas.

"I hired a new ranch manager," said Byron. There was a glow in his eyes, as if he was keeping a secret.

"So, you can spend plenty of time in Seattle?" The hopeful note was clear in Devin's voice.

Instead of answering, Byron looked to Lucas. "Steve called me."

Lucas frowned, his eyes narrowing. "What did he want?"

"Out."

Lucas cocked his head to one side.

"Out of what?" Devin asked.

"Pacific Robotics," Lexi squealed.

"No way." But a slow smile was forming on Lucas's face. "You didn't."

"The hell I didn't," said Byron. "He seems to think he's going to take South America by storm. He was looking for a quick sale to raise the capital, and I gave it to him."

"It has to be approved by the Board," Lucas drawled.

"I'm pretty sure I'll have Amelia's support," said Byron. The toddler adored her Uncle Byron. "And we brought you a bottle of Macallan Fine and Rare, 1926. Just in case we had to grease the skids."

Lucas grinned. "I'm liking your chances."

"Does this mean what I think it means?" Devin was getting impatient.

Lucas tugged her close, tucking her against his body and kissing her temple. "It means, they're going to live here in Seattle. Byron's going to be my business partner, and we're all going to live happily ever after."

* * * * *